INFECTION IN THE MIND

DOCTOR WISE BOOK 10

ARJAY LEWIS

MIND
BENDER
PRESS

Cover Design: Marianne Nowicki, PremadeEbookCoverShop.com
Editing: Libby Broadbent

ISBN-13: 978-1734229141
ISBN-10: 1734229144

Published by:
Mindbender Press
474 South Main Street
Phillipsburg NJ 08865
www.mindbenderpress.com

DEDICATION

To Patricia Wolven
"Patti"
A helluva lady and
a big fan of Leonard Wise.

"Fear is a disease that eats away at logic and makes man inhuman."

—Marian Anderson

"We are infected by our own misunderstanding of how our own minds work."

—Kevin Kelly

PROLOGUE

Ziya was an artist.

Not just a scientist, and far more than merely a chemist, he was a man who took living cells and sculpted masterpieces of doomsday.

He was surrounded by the tools of his art: microscopes, bunsen burners, culture dishes, dissection pans, and sealed cages where infected test rats lurked.

He checked the seals on several canisters, giving them a final wipe with disinfectant.

He carefully removed the hood and detached the breathing unit from his hazmat suit. The exhaust fan in his lab had been running for hours so the air smelled fresh with the aroma of strong cleaners. He'd spent hours cleaning every surface in preparation for his guests.

He pulled on a new pair of nitrile gloves just as there was a knock at the door.

"Come in," he yelled with his thick Romanian accent.

A thin man with a crew cut peeked in. "Is it safe?" he asked with a Southern drawl.

"Yes, yes, I have been cleaning for hours. I knew you were coming," Ziya gushed.

Today he would get his money and leave. His lab had been the center of his life for many long weeks, and it was time to move on.

The door flew open and four men and two women entered, all fit, each wearing camouflage military outfits and heavy gloves.

A bearded man nodded at the four large canisters. "Will it work?"

Ziya fought a wave of revulsion. Beards, he shuddered. Collectors of dead skin cells and oil from the skin. Breeding grounds for bacteria, yeast, and every other microorganism imaginable. Ziya shaved every part of his body, even his head and eyebrows. To have a beard, all that filth right under your mouth, was abhorrent.

"Will it work?" Ziya repeated with his thick accent. "It was tricky, I had to suspend the virus in tanks of liquid nitrogen. When released into the air, when the virus becomes warm, it will do its work. You are not getting a weapon, you are getting a portrait of death."

One of the other men spoke to the bearded leader. "Y'all sure gas masks will protect us?"

Ziya nodded and opened a trunk to reveal six gas masks. "I modified them. They will work, even with direct exposure."

The bearded man smiled. "Good."

Ziya frowned. "You do understand how the canisters function?"

"Yeah, we ain't stupid," the blond man said.

The others chuckled.

The bearded man raised a hand and the group quieted. "Yeah, I knew we had to get atomizers that could release it slowly. It'll discharge in small bursts so the frozen liquid won't clog up the spray."

"On a timer?" Ziya asked.

"Just like you told me."

"I am sorry I could not have the atomizers for you today."

"We got that handled," the bearded man assured him. "Check your account, you'll find the money is there. Let's move it out, men."

The three other men and the women collected their masks, one at a time.

One of the women spoke, and Ziya noticed there was something odd about her eyes, but he couldn't tell what it was from where he stood. She ordered the others to collect the canisters. A tall man with a scar on his head picked up one canister and easily flipped it up onto his shoulder.

The two men carried one canister and the women left with another held between them. Only the bearded leader remained with the final canister.

Ziya checked his phone and smiled broadly.

"You got your money?"

"Yes, this is good, very good," he said and turned to face his buyer. "I believe you Americans say, 'it was pleasure doing business with you'."

The bearded man didn't offer to shake hands. "What are you going to do when we set these off?"

"Do?" Ziya smiled. "I will be gone, the lab closed. You told me you are detonating them here in New Jersey. I will be back in Romania."

"And you're okay with the fact that you will be the cause of a pandemic?" the man asked with raised eyebrows.

"You don't understand. I have spent my life learning about poisons, viruses and creating new forms of them. You wish to bring your god's wrath on people who do not believe the way you do. I take god's creations and help them become the weapons of such wrath."

The man nodded. "There will be a purging, my friend. This country will be better because of it. The survivors will build a new America. I just have to clean up any loose ends."

He turned and headed for the door.

"By the way… you are one of those loose ends."

Ziya turned to face the bearded man across the room. The man wore his gas mask and stood next to the canister, a gun pointed in Ziya's direction.

There was a loud "thwack" and Ziya fell into his chair, pain overwhelming him. He fought for breath as he looked down to see a red stain blossoming on his chest.

As Ziya watched, too stunned to move, the blond man returned with a glass jar filled with amber liquid and a rag protruding from the top. He passed it to the leader and grabbed the final canister.

Removing his mask and reaching into his pocket, the bearded man extracted a lighter.

"I will see that they glorify your name, Ziya Stanislaw, that I promise you."

He lit the rag and threw the flaming jar in as he shut the door.

Fire bloomed over the concrete floor, and Ziya thought how beautiful it looked as brushstrokes of flames splattered against him.

He was an artist. Death was, indeed, his masterpiece.

1. COERCED CONDITION

"One more," the woman in blue scrubs demanded.

I lifted my right leg as high as I could against the elastic band. With a groan, I slowly lowered it back to the footrest of my wheelchair.

"I think that's enough for today," Sheryl told me, in that annoying perky voice.

"Thanks, Sheryl," I muttered.

"Don't be such a gloomy Gus, Mister Wise! You just have to build those muscles." She picked up her clipboard and made some notes.

I sighed. I had told her it was "Doctor Wise" or "Len" repeatedly, but that information never seemed to stick. I had to admit, she was a good physical therapist, a job referred to as PT at the hospital. Those of us who had to go through it called it Pain and Torture.

A little over a week ago, I had surgery to correct my fused right leg. This was a gift paid for by my brain surgeon father, who knew an orthopedic specialist who felt he could repair the damage from my car accident over eight years earlier.

When they pulled me out of the wreckage, my legs had been very badly damaged. Then again, I made out better than my fiancée, Cathy.

She ended up dead.

Due to the extensive damage to my leg and knee, the doctors at the time had felt that fusing the leg was the only choice. My father's friend, Doctor Irving Hirschfeld, decided he could reconstruct the knee and that with therapy, the muscles could support my weight. This required removing the metal rods, and basically breaking the leg where the femur had been fused to the tibia.

And the thigh bone's connected to the knee bone...

Eight years of not bending the knee, since I had no knee to bend, had left me with terribly weak muscles that were a multitude of scar tissue. Since this recent surgery, my leg hurt so damn much that in retrospect, I wondered why I even agreed to it.

It didn't really make sense to have surgery in the middle of the school year, but the opportunity to have two good working legs was too much of a temptation, and I agreed. Next week, I would be getting back to my classes at Garden State University, where I worked as an Associate Professor in the Parapsychology Department.

That department consisted of one professor — me — and one Teacher's Assistant, Theodoré Santos, who had covered my classes for the last week. Teaching the concepts and history of parapsychology, Extrasensory Perception, and the world of the invisible is a challenge, but I had a great teacher who I'd studied with, and I experienced it all first-hand.

Psychic visions, precognition, even telepathy were things I knew well and intimately. I had to teach in a way that focused on the science, as few of my students would ever have the abilities that were commonplace to me. It was like trying to teach music theory and composition to people who have never heard music.

For the last week, in a haze of pain-killers, my abilities had not been functioning. Any kind of mind-altering substance — a drink of alcohol or cheap marijuana — blocked my mind from perceiving the flow of psychic data that was all around me, all the time.

When I first started having psychic insights, the experiences had been unwanted, and I had pushed them away through the liberal use of alcohol. After a few years, as my abilities increased, so did my drinking until I became a full-blown alcoholic.

Luckily, I found a teacher who helped me control my mind, and I joined AA to control my drinking. I was using the painkillers as little as I could bear as I didn't want an opiate addiction on top of it all.

However, due to the drugs, it had been a very peaceful week, and I was ready to get back to my classes. If nothing else, it would give me something to focus on other than my damn leg.

I managed to stand as Sheryl helped me on with my winter coat, a long black wool thing that went down to my knees. Being six-foot-four, it was a 44 Long, so the sleeves and the length was enough to cover me. I was dressed in a black track suit, with three white lines down the arms and the sides of my legs. If I joined a marathon, I'd look at home. But it was February in New Jersey and not a time for marathons, or most outdoor activities other than skiing or sledding, and there had been little snow.

With my coat in place, and lowered back in the chair, Sheryl told me to keep doing my exercises and she'd see me next week.

I steered the wheelchair to the elevator. Since I only needed it for the first few weeks it was a rental with a large plastic tube carrier attached to the back. The tube held my trusty cobra head cane which I needed for support when I stood.

I hadn't been doing a lot of standing, except in physical therapy.

As I rolled out the front doors of the hospital, I saw my van in the lot. Fortunately, the accelerator and brake controls were operated with my hands, so I was still able to drive with my leg in its current state.

Did I mention that it hurt? Especially after therapy.

My smart phone rang, and I stopped to struggle it out of my pocket. The screen lit up: Lt. McGee.

"Hey Bill," I said as I answered the device, a cloud of vapor rising from my mouth.

"How's therapy going?"

A part of me wanted to yell, "Great, I went from having a limp to being stuck in a rolling chair."

Instead, I muttered, "Hurts like Hell. What's up?"

"We've been requested to assist the FBI New Jersey Task Force."

I sighed, annoyance creeping into my voice. "What do *they* want?"

"They wouldn't tell me, said it had to be explained at a meeting — in one hour, here at Mountainview PD."

I rolled up to the driver's door of my van. "Christ, Bill, I just got out of therapy. All I want to do is go back to bed. Can you find out what it's about and brief me?"

"I can't. Apparently it's a very big deal. Can you make it?"

"I don't see why they even need me, Bill. I'm just a civilian consultant, not a cop."

"That's the thing, Len. Some big guys in Washington asked Gabe Petrie for both of us by name."

Gabe Petrie was the head of the FBI New Jersey Task Force and not one of my biggest fans. I had upstaged him once or twice and he didn't like it.

I frowned. "Really? I wasn't aware that anyone in Washington even knew we existed."

"It appears they do. I'll see you in an hour."

Bill ended the call before I could argue, which annoyed me further.

I opened the door of my van. The built-in lift turned out and lowered the driver's seat. I pushed myself up with my cane and sat in the upholstered chair. I opened the side door, and heaved the wheelchair into the space behind the driver's seat. There was a button on the side of the lift, which once pressed, raised and turned me to face forward in the driver position. Another button shut all the doors and I was ready to go.

I was trying to decide if I should just show up in my track suit, sweaty, or go home and attempt to shower. I hadn't shaved in a week, so my face was covered in bristles. I would love to say I could pull off the sexy three-day beard look, but it just made me appear sloppy.

In the end, I just drove to MPD. If I couldn't catch a break a week after surgery, then screw it.

Forty minutes after the phone call, I wheeled my way into the back entrance of the Mountainview Police Department using my magnetic ID card to let myself in. I didn't bother going to Bill's office but made my way to the large conference room and texted him to let him know I'd arrived.

The big man burst into the room a minute after I sent the text. I'm tall, but thin and lithe. Bill isn't. He's about 6'6" and built like a fullback, with broad shoulders and well-developed muscles.

"Can I get you anything, Len? Coffee?" Bill asked.

"That would be great," I said and smiled. A few months earlier, I solved a case for MPD and had received a reward for my success. I made it a point to buy one of those fancy single cup coffeemakers for the MPD as a gift. Considering how much time I spent there, and how much of the lousy cop coffee I'd had to drink, it was an investment in my own stomach-lining.

Bill returned carrying a styrofoam cup for me as well as one for himself. "Have I thanked you lately for the coffeemaker?"

I took a sip. He'd added a little cream, and it was good. "Every time I come by. Believe me, it benefits me as much as anyone else."

"Nice to know you two can show up on time, when requested." Gabe Petrie stood in the doorway, a short man with wide shoulders, and an arrogant look on his face.

As he stepped into the room, Doctor Kate Yearling appeared behind him. The hair of her fiery wig matched her equally ginger eyebrows.

I smiled. "Kate? I didn't know you'd be here."

She stepped into the room, her frame was still a little too thin, but she'd made a lot of progress lately.

She walked up to my wheelchair, a smile on her face. "How's the leg?"

I gave an enigmatic shrug. "You know, physical therapy hurts like hell."

"Oh, I know," she said and grimaced. "Even months after the 'incident' every stupid thing they had me do hurt."

Nine months ago, Kate had attempted to track down a serial killer. The fiend had removed her hair and the first layer of her scalp with a scalpel. The fact that she survived at all had been a miracle, and with the wig, she nearly resembled her old self.

We had been lovers since December.

She glanced to make sure that Gabe was speaking to Bill, and leaned close to whisper, "When do I get to try out the new and improved Leonard Wise?"

This got a raised eyebrow from me. She had spent the night with me the day before I went into surgery and had driven me to the hospital.

"I thought you told me we were keeping things casual?"

She shrugged. "We are. I just *casually* want to see how you are with two good legs."

I peeked over at Gabe and Bill who had their backs to us and were going over a report together.

"I'm afraid at this point, you would have to do all the work," I suggested.

This earned me a small smile. "I think I'm fine with that."

She leaned back, our intimate moment over. She put on her "game-face" and returned to the men.

I watched Kate. She was a good-looking woman, and I was one of the few people with whom she was comfortable taking off the wig and allowing me to see the criss-crossed network of skin grafts on the top of her head. When we came together and made love on the previous Christmas, we were both fragile and needy. It was a reaffirmation of life, and we'd both enjoyed it.

We'd been seeing each other sporadically, often at the last minute when we were both free. Yet we also shied away from each other a bit, as if both of us were cautious of revealing more than we were comfortable to share.

But the sex was good.

I wheeled over to join the group at the conference table. Gabe had laid out a map of Essex County, and was highlighting something in pen.

"Didn't they even give you a clue about what they found?" Bill asked.

"Not even a hint," Gabe grumbled. "I asked them, and I don't understand why we're being kept in the dark."

The phone on the wall, which was also an intercom, buzzed. Bill pressed a button on the front of it. "This is McGee."

"Lieutenant, the guests you were expecting have arrived," announced the voice of CeeCee Carter, our dispatcher.

"Buzz them in, please."

There was the sound of a nearby buzzer a few doors down the hall, and the click of the outer door being opened.

We all moved so we could face the door to see who had come up from Washington, requesting for us to be part of their investigation.

Two men strode into the room, both looking very FBI. They were tall, both in dark suits, one man white and the other black. The white man had a receding hairline and a widow's peak. His African American partner looked as if he'd stepped out of a fitness magazine, with a strong chin, shaved head, and Hollywood good looks.

For me, it was as if they didn't even exist.

An equally tall African-American woman followed them into the room, her skin a dark patina, her hair tied back in a professional style.

Jyanette Emery. My old girlfriend.

The woman I adored and still loved.

She moved into the room purposefully, and my heart felt like it stopped beating as I stared at her.

I knew every inch of her glorious frame. We'd spent many nights in each other's arms, professing our love physically as well as emotionally.

She'd become pregnant with my child, but the baby had been ripped from her womb because of a monster bent on revenge against me.

She'd left town and moved to Virginia. I had learned she was hired by the Department of Justice in Washington, but I hadn't known she was working as a field agent.

Her eyes swept the room, until her gaze rested on me in the wheelchair. Time slowed, and I watched several reactions flow across her face, all at once. The first was surprise, and I could see that she was concerned that I was in a wheelchair. The second was a flash of anger. She'd always warned me that my involvement in police business would get me crippled or killed. The final was wonder, as she saw that my right leg was bent, my crippled knee repaired.

I felt like an idiot; unshaven, in a track suit, still wearing my winter coat, with my mouth hanging open in shock and surprise.

"I'm Agent Marsh and this is Agent Calvin," the tall white guy stated, pulling me out of my reverie and back into real time. "We're with the FBI Joint Terrorism Task Force."

Petrie spoke up, "The JTTF? Here?"

"This is General Counsel Attorney, Jyanette Emery." Calvin indicated Jyanette. "We understand you have worked with Ms. Emery in the past."

Bill stepped forward. "I'm Lieutenant McGee, and yes we know OGC Emery quite well." Bill nodded at my former lover. "Good to see you, Jyanette."

"Likewise, Lieutenant," Jyanette said in a clipped tone, her eyes glancing to me, as if trying to process the situation.

"Gentleman, I'm Director Petrie," Gabe said. "And this is my profiler, Doctor Kate Yearling."

The two men nodded to Kate who returned it. I saw her glance at Jyanette and then at me, her jaw tightening, as annoyance flashed in her eyes.

Gabe went on, "You want to tell me why you called us here, and told us nothing?"

Calvin threw his shoulders back, making him look even taller. "We have reason to believe that Mountainview might be the center of a terrorist attack."

The room fell silent.

2. HEART AFFLICTION

"What exactly does that mean?" grumbled Gabe, when he could speak again. "What do those map coordinates you sent have to do with a terrorist attack?"

Marsh stepped over to the map. "One week ago, there was a fire at a warehouse at those coordinates. Turns out that it contained a laboratory."

Bill looked at the map. "That's right on the border of Mountainview and Bloomdale. In a warehouse, you say?"

Calvin nodded. "Fortunately, the lab area was sealed so the fire didn't spread. But there was a burnt corpse inside, as well as cages of animals... also dead."

Marsh piped up. "We were lucky that once the fire was under control, the Fire Captain was smart enough to call in the FBI. The warehouse was secured, and a hazmat team was brought in, along with a portable lab."

Gabe Petrie's jaw set. "I take it what you found was not reassuring."

"Not at all," Marsh went on. "The animals didn't die in the fire. They died from a disease. Best as the lab guys have been able to ascertain, they were infected with a cross between the virus that creates Dengue Fever and the bacteria from a strain of tuberculosis."

"What?" Petrie gasped.

Marsh went on. "The dead man found on the scene was Ziya Stanislaw, chemist and mercenary, well-known for concocting designer poisons for whoever is willing to pay."

Petrie shook his head. "Hasn't the Bureau been trying to track him down for years?"

"He was high on our list, but the lab was a first-class set up," Calvin asserted. "Everything a mad scientist could need."

"Needless to say, in the past week, ever since we discovered this lab, the FBI have pulled together a full team devoted to trying to find out more about this virus that killed the animals," Marsh added.

"You think he created it?" Petrie fretted. "How?"

"We believe he had full sequence-verified DNA fragments created by several suppliers, and was able to infect a drug-resistant variant of tuberculous with the virus. He then used the animals to create and test this new strain, using their blood and a stable culture to grow more of it."

"Our team found tanks of liquid nitrogen on site," Calvin explained. "But they were empty."

Marsh looked over the crowd. "There was also a contraption connected to one of the nitrogen tanks to fill smaller ones. It had a side container that allowed something to be added."

"Is that common?" McGee asked.

Calvin spoke up. "Very *un*common. Viruses are often stored in sterile containers in a bath of liquid nitrogen, however, there have been cases where the nitrogen became infected when a glass ampule containing a virus shattered in a storage case."

"Liquid nitrogen is like, three hundred degrees below zero," I interjected. "Wouldn't that kill this bacteria or the virus?"

"Surprisingly, no," Marsh said. "There have been reported cases of entire storage vats becoming infectious because of a single broken ampule."

Calvin turned from his partner. "We believe Mr. Stanislaw used this concept to create tanks of liquid nitrogen contaminated by this pathogen he'd created."

Marsh said, "The scientists tell me that if there was a way to release the liquid slowly and warm it, it could infect people through airborne transmission."

"We think the reason Stanislaw combined the Dengue Fever virus with the tuberculous bacteria was so that it would directly attack the lungs. In an enclosed space, you can see the dangers this creates."

Kate spoke up. "Dengue Fever only has a fatality rate of about two-and-a-half percent."

Marsh nodded. "That's the stats for the original virus which is spread through mosquitos. However, we believe this airborne hybrid could be fatal in over fifty percent of the cases."

We all sat in stunned silence.

"We are operating from the theory that this was created for a client," Marsh pointed out.

Calvin spoke up. "Since Stanislaw had been shot and the fire in the lab was started with an accelerant, we are working from the belief that the buyer has taken delivery."

"Wait a minute," Bill said. "This happened *here*, in *my* town?"

"Yes," Marsh nodded. "We believe that the buyer thought Mountainview would be an ideal location to unleash a biological weapon."

I finally had my wits about me enough to speak up. "Why here?"

"That's obvious," Kate interjected. "A college town, trains and buses going into Manhattan. If they could infect college students, young people, the resulting panic would be crushing."

"Plus, with people attempting to escape," Marsh's tone was dry, "they could easily spread the virus throughout the country through person-to-person contact."

"The legal ramifications alone are unthinkable," Jyanette explained. "The DOJ has called in every asset and we believe we may have a lead on who the buyer might be."

"Since the lab was destroyed and Ziya shot," Marsh added. "We believe we have a limited window of opportunity to stop a possible attack."

Calvin looked the group over. "We asked all of you to be involved because of your success in stopping a previous terrorist incident last September."

I nodded. Agent Calvin was speaking of an attack from former hypnotherapist, Anika Vanya. She had concocted an insane plan to blow up a data facility located in the Elizabeth Seaport which housed electronic information regarding police and financial records. Wiping it out would have affected cities up and down the entire East Coast. We stopped her, but at a cost.

I lost Jyanette because of that incident.

Now Jyanette stood in the same room as me, as tall and beautiful as I recalled. She looked much stronger and healthier than when she moved to Virginia the previous September.

"Our lead came from surveillance footage from around the warehouse, mostly vehicles that came and went," Calvin explained. "A team has been going through traffic cam footage to find anything to identify the group that hired Ziya."

Jyanette spoke up. "We traced one pickup truck seen leaving the area with tanks of compressed gas, and the DOJ believes that the buyer is a loosely associated group known as the Faction."

"Aren't they white supremacists?" Bill asked.

"Yeah, a bunch of Neo-Nazis that are more clowns than criminals," Gabe observed. "My task force has kept an eye on them. They have get-togethers and so-called 'training sessions', but nothing overt where we could move in and bust them. We aren't even sure of all of their followers, and have only identified the top members of the group."

Marsh said. "They've been staying low-key for a reason. What research we've been able to do suggests that they had been doing a massive fund-raising drive, and we think that's how the lab was financed."

"Last we were aware," Gabe said, "they were out in the Western part of the state, nowhere near Mountainview."

"As it turns out," Marsh said, "we eventually lost track of the pickup truck, and haven't been able to discover their trail or where those canisters ended up."

Calvin turned to face me. "We're interested in anything that Doctor Wise can contribute."

All eyes were on me.

"Um... I'll help in any way I can," I muttered, overwhelmed both by the situation and the almost-hypnotic presence of Jyanette.

"We don't have to tell you, Doctor, that time is of the essence," Calvin said, as he opened the satchel he'd been carrying and extracted several photographs. He passed them out to the others in the room. "This is Joseph Lindwall. We believe he is the current leader of the Faction."

Kate glanced at the photo and handed it to me. It showed a tall man in a camouflage outfit holding an AR-15. He was bearded and posed in front of a large rock, looking into the distance as if on a Messianic journey.

"I've seen his file," Kate told the others. "Controlling father, raised with anti-Semitic views. He was a member of the KKK but left because they were too 'soft' for him. Started his own group. Acts like he's had military training, but never joined the armed services. Lots of anger and resentment, and he blames people of color and Jews for the failures in his life."

"What we need in the immediate," Marsh said, "is to set up a base of operations. Lieutenant, if we could take over this conference room, get our people in here—"

"What's wrong with the NJ Task Force offices?" Gabe argued.

"Too far from the action," Marsh pointed out. "Morris Plains is over half an hour away."

Calvin nodded. "Plus, we need the large parking lot here. It gives us a staging area for portable labs and our strike teams."

"And your lot is out of sight from the main street, away from prying eyes," Marsh added. "We need to be here to protect the town and stop these guys."

"What if you can't?" I questioned.

Calvin and Marsh exchanged a look. Marsh spoke up, "Then we have to isolate and quarantine the town. No one in, no one out."

"People will die," I said.

"Then we'd better stop the Faction before they release that stuff," Calvin intoned solemnly.

The meeting lasted another hour, with not only a strategy for finding members of the Faction, but also plans to shut down the trains and lock down the town if necessary.

The idea alone was a nightmare.

I was still aching from the PT and distracted by Jyanette. Finally, I excused myself, and rolled out to the bathroom. Alone in the tiled room, I was able to use my cane so I could stand to do my business.

As I headed back to the conference room, Jyanette approached me in the hall.

"Hello, Len," she said haltingly.

I cleared my throat as I gazed up at her, my heart feeling like it was being torn from my chest and stomped on. I forced a smile. "Jyanette. It's… nice to see you. You… um… look good."

I felt like an idiot. Small talk is tough enough, but it's almost impossible when you're overwhelmed by passion for a woman you want with every fiber of your being.

The attraction was just as strong as it had been. The months had done nothing to subdue my ardor or lessen the pain of losing her.

"You have a right knee," Jyanette observed. "I mean, your leg can bend."

"Chanukah present from my father," I mumbled. "A surgeon owed him a favor. He paid for it all."

She brightened at this. "Oh, that's good. I mean, you and your parents had that falling out and all."

"How's your family? Are Deka and George good?"

"My parents, fine, fine. Dad's working on a restoration of a 1787 structure, having a good time."

"Your sisters?"

"Natisha's getting married, finally. She's lived with that man for four years. And Shanika just told us that she's gay."

"Oh?"

"Yeah. I kind of knew anyway. I mean, all the signs were there," she said.

She stood looking down at me, the pair of us just staring at each other. All I wanted was to get up out of the chair and take her in my arms.

Finally, Jyanette said, "I guess we'd better get back in there."

I put my head down and wheeled into the room. As I entered followed by Jyanette, Kate shot a look at us, and did not appear happy.

As the agents went on about the plans for quarantine, Bill announced that he had to leave the room to speak to Captain Harris and get approval for the FBI to use the conference room.

He returned a few minutes later. The request was approved, and at the captain's suggestion, Bill would meet with local Mayor Stewart's office, to arrange a time for her to be briefed.

I needed to get out of there, as the pain-killers I'd taken that day had worn off. Not only did my leg hurt more, but mental impressions were beginning to hammer at my mind.

Mental energy is increased by strong emotions of anxiety, fear, hate, and the like. Everyone in that room was concerned about a possible disaster, so those intense thoughts were flying all about.

This data won't track them down…

Does everyone get how much danger we're in…

Right here, in Mountainview…

Emotions swirled around me, overwhelming and invasive. I just wanted to shut it all out, but it was difficult. Tired and in pain, my mental barriers were not strong enough to keep these thoughts and images at bay.

I grabbed one of the photos, told the agents that I needed to work on my contribution on my own, and headed for the door.

"Gentleman, I need to consult with Doctor Wise before he leaves," Kate said, as she moved over to grab my wheelchair and push me out of the room.

"I can handle it myself," I told her as she pushed the chair toward the exit.

"You looked tired," Kate comforted me. "I imagine the mental state of the group was getting to you."

I always forgot how perceptive Kate was.

"Yeah, it was," I said. I pulled my winter coat back on as we headed out to the parking lot. "I also think I can do better alone. If I get any hits, I'll call the team."

"I figured," Kate said as we reached my vehicle. She stood in front of me and leaned forward to be eye level. "I was thinking I could come by after dinner, maybe even around nine or ten."

I think my eyes grew wide before I responded. "Kate, that's not a good idea—"

Her face changed as anger flared in her eyes. She folded her arms across her chest. "It's *her*, isn't it?"

For a psychic, I don't have much of a poker face.

"Kate, you know how I feel about Jyanette," I argued, annoyed that I was stuck in this situation.

She rose to her full height. "What are you going to do when she finishes this case and goes back to DC?"

"Look, I'm not in a good place—"

"Oh, the utter *crap!*" Kate scoffed. "I'm not interested in your mind, Wise. But suit yourself! Go ahead and moon over your *'great lost love*.'"

She stormed off, as I sat there wanting to say or do something, but not having any clue what.

I liked Kate and didn't want to hurt her feelings, but I was still in love with Jyanette and being in the same room with her was devastating.

I went through the arduous task of getting myself and my wheelchair into the van and headed home.

I share a beautiful Victorian house on a cul-de-sac in Mountainview with Mrs. Higgins, a former cook to the wealthy. She bought the house with cash on my advice, and then offered to rent me the "mother" section of her mother/daughter home.

I appreciated it more than ever as I parked the van in the circular driveway and headed for my separate entrance. The main entrance has only a few stone steps, but that was a problem with the wheelchair. My sitting room and bedroom were an extension built onto the original structure, with an entrance at ground-level.

I was tired and hungry, and hoped that some food and maybe coffee would wake me up enough to try to do a reading on the leader of the Faction.

I had placed the photo the FBI agents had given me in the pocket of my wheelchair and hoped I could use it as a way to focus my mind.

On the down-side, it meant no pain killers until after.

I wheeled into the kitchen to find Mrs. Higgins, her short frame clothed in an apron, as she pushed one of her graying auburn tresses out of her face.

"Oh, Doctor, ye're home, then," she announced with her Irish brogue. "Ye needn't have come all the way oop here, I would bring ye something to eat."

I smiled, as I always did when I saw my landlady. "Mrs. Higgins, you're not a servant. You are the lady of the manse, and it's rude for me to expect—"

"Hush now!" she demanded. "Ye've been through surgery, and ye've exhausted yerself with that physical therapy. Why'd ye take so long to get home, I expected ye hours ago?"

"I've been called into a case," I said and met her eyes.

"It's more than that, I think."

Suddenly my throat was tight, and I felt as if a dam was about to burst. "Jyanette was there."

I lowered my head, as a single tear fell unexpectedly, and I was too overwhelmed to speak. Mrs. Higgins moved to a paper towel dispenser on the wall, pulled one, and handed it to me. I wiped my eye and blew my nose, the wave of grief passing as I regained control.

"There, there, now," she said. "That moost have been a shock to ye."

"Sorry," I mumbled.

"For what?" she said, her voice calm. "For feelin' too much, or lovin' too deep? No, Doctor, that's not a thing to apologize for. Ye loved Jyanette with all yer heart, wanted to be with her, and raise yer child."

I sat there in abject misery. "It's just seeing her again... it was like a punch in the gut."

"Did she speak to ye?"

"In the hall for a minute or so. It was... awkward. We were meeting with FBI agents."

"FBI?" she said solemnly. "Then it's something bad?"

"It could be a terrorist attack, right here in Mountainview."

Her eyes grew wide. "I see. Do ye think ye can help?"

"I'm going to try."

"Weel then, let's get ye back into your room, and I'll bring ye some bread and a nice soup, all right?"

She pulled my wheelchair out through the swinging door into the hall.

"Thanks, Mrs. Higgins," I said, willing to let her wheel me.

"Yer still recovering, and there's a life-or-death case and Jyanette there and all. I'd be surprised if ye weren't thrown a bit."

She opened the door to my sitting room and wheeled me to my desk before turning to the bathroom, and I heard the sound of running water. "Now then, I've started a bath fer ye. Ye sit right here, and oy'll bring ye something to eat."

She wandered back to the kitchen as I pulled the photo of the leader of the Faction from the side pocket of my chair. The posed picture had him looking off into the distance, but I could see that Joseph Lindwall had cold eyes indeed.

The impression I received was, while he peered into the distance, he searched for only one thing.

Death.

3. ROMANTIC DISORDER

Mrs. Higgins was as good as her word. As my tub filled she brought me a bowl of hearty soup, with crusty bread and a cup of coffee, as I "needed a wee boost".

The meal was fantastic, and I managed to get myself undressed, and into the hot bath, which was also heavenly. I kept my right leg elevated out of the water, as I examined the stitches, marveling at the expertise that had been used to make them. My original calling was to be a surgeon, like my father. I excelled in my studies, as well as surgical technique. The stitches Doctor Hirschfeld made on my leg were tight and perfectly spaced. Such accuracy could only be learned from years of practice, and it reflected his skill.

I considered the scarring from the car accident, and the fact that my right leg was thinner than my left. The muscles had been badly damaged, some of the mass removed, and several of the muscles had not been used much once the leg had been fused.

It was interesting to assess my own leg like a spectator. I hadn't become a surgeon. The death of my fiancée and the awakening of my psychic abilities had sent my life down another path.

I got out of the tub and stood on my one good leg until I'd dried myself. Then I returned to my chair, wheeled into the bedroom, and dressed in pajamas.

Why not? I wasn't going anywhere.

I wanted to do a reading of Lindwall's photo and see if I could get anything. Then I would take a painkiller and go to bed.

I rolled out to the sitting room just as my phone jingled, and I saw on the screen it was Kate.

"Hey, Kate."

"I wanted you to know the meetings are done. We want to reconvene tomorrow at oh-eight-hundred."

"I'll be there."

"I… want to apologize," she said.

"Kate, that's not necessary," I sighed. "I was just…"

We fell into an uneasy silence.

"It's not that late," she suggested. "I could still come by."

"I've got to do a reading on this Lindwall guy. Then, I'm going to bed."

"Okay, I get it."

"It's not you Kate, it's me."

"A line both men *and* women hate to hear."

"Right now, I have to get to work on my contribution to this case. I'll see you in the morning, Kate."

"Good hunting, Len."

I ended the call and stared at my phone. Kate had never treated our sexual liaisons as anything serious. She did enjoy spending the night, but I was beginning to suspect she may have started to feel more for me than she let on.

Who was I kidding? I liked Kate, respected her, enjoyed her, but when Jyanette walked into that room, no one else mattered, what I felt for anyone else wasn't important.

The one thing, the *only* thing was Jyanette.

What would I do when she left? Mope around for a few weeks and get on with my life.

Shrugging off my self-pity, I prepared to use whatever abilities I possessed to try to locate Mr. Lindwall.

I pulled the chair up to my desk and stared at the photo. He was carefully posed to reflect strength and a sense of purpose.

I took a deep breath, closed my eyes, and let it out slowly. Then I began to focus on my breathing, to allow myself to sink into an alpha state.

In… out. In… out.

I placed my hand on the photo. Everything has an energy, and photographs carry a slight imprint of the subject or location. I needed to try to find *his* energy and attempt to locate him, wherever he was.

I focused and reached out, my hand atop the photograph.

I heard voices, speaking in the darkness, far away, barely discernible.

I concentrated and tried to keep myself out of the way, listening.

"Maybe burning the lab was a bad choice," a voice was saying.

"Not at all," a gruff voice replied. "It was sure to kill any samples, so they can't find a cure."

"Yep," another voice, not as deep, said with a Southern twang. "With them firemen there and all that water, it probably got rid of any trace evidence we mighta left."

I began to see lights and images as they coalesced around me, forming into a long, narrow room, where three men were seated at a table. The space appeared small, and the roof low. I felt a need to duck my head, even though I wasn't really there physically.

Two of the three men at the table were heavily muscled, the third was skinny. The light came from a small oil lamp in the middle of the table. The skinny one was blond, one was a dark haired man with a scar over his eye, and the third had a bearded face that I recognized at once: Joseph Lindwall.

In front of them were three glasses and a bottle filled with an amber liquid.

I tried to look around the strange room. There appeared to be cabinets on the walls, and an area in the back separated with an accordion-style door.

"I don't see why we have to wait," the man with the scar complained. "We set the canisters into the locations and get the hell out of here."

Lindwall spoke with the gruff voice I had heard earlier. "We need the timers to release the virus slowly. It's in liquid nitrogen, and if it's released all at once the atomizers will freeze up. It's got to be released in slow bursts. Besides, we don't want to be anywhere near those canisters when they go off. We want to be on the other side of the country."

The blond man smirked. "California, here we come!"

"Wyoming," the scarred man corrected him. "We don't want to be near crowds of people."

"Brothers." Lindwall raised his glass. "We will be making this *our* country again."

The three men stood, held up their glasses, toasted each other, and downed the liquor.

The man with the scar looked at Lindwall. "Are you sure Tommy will be up to the job?"

"I trust Tommy with my life," Lindwall replied.

I had no idea who Tommy was, or even who the two men with Lindwall were. I turned to examine the room. It was so dark, even in my non-physical form, I couldn't see clearly. Then I caught a silhouette on the other end of the long room: a steering wheel?

I realized this wasn't a room at all, but a large recreational vehicle which included living quarters. That's why everything was so tight. They had parked the vehicle somewhere off the beaten path, as I could detect no lights through the windshield in the front. The only light in the room was that oil lamp.

There was a knocking as I turned back to the men, but the scene was fading around me. The insistent rapping pulled me out of my altered state.

I raised my head, still seated at my desk as the knocking continued on the outer door, my private entrance into the house. Anger flooded me. I'd gotten a glimpse of Lindwall and his cohorts, but had not found anything to pinpoint their location, other than the fact that they were in an RV.

"I'm coming!" I barked at the person knocking on my door, my annoyance growing. It was probably Kate, who certainly was not one to take no for an answer.

I rolled to the door and undid the lock. As I flung open the door I growled, "Dammit Kate, I told you that I—"

Jyanette stood in the doorway, a winter coat cloaking her tall frame.

I literally was so shocked I almost choked on my words. I sat there, stunned, my mouth hanging open as a cold breeze rushed in around her.

"May I come in?" she asked.

This got my brain functioning again. "Oh yes, of course."

I rolled my chair out of the way and she strode in. I shut the door and looked up at her.

She smiled. "I guess you weren't expecting me."

"Absolutely not," I muttered, struggling to keep control of myself. I was shocked, true, but also thrilled that she was there.

"So, you and Kate, huh?" she remarked.

This caught me off guard and annoyance crept into my voice. "I don't think that's any of your business."

She opened her coat and looked down at me, I could read nothing from the expression on her face. I was puzzled that she didn't take the coat off completely and hang it on the coatrack behind the door. She knew where it was from the many nights she had stayed with me.

"You're right, it's not. Though I guess that answers my question."

A flash of anger rushed through me. "Is that why you're here? To inquire about my love life? Look, Kate and I were two lonely people who found a little comfort—"

She raised her hands in a pose of surrender. "Len, you don't have to explain yourself to me."

This calmed me down. "Oh... okay."

"I can't stay. I just wanted to talk to you for a minute, without the craziness of all those people around us."

I pulled my cane from its holder on the side of the wheelchair and used it to push myself to my feet.

Jyanette looked concerned. "Should you be doing that?"

"I'm a little tired of looking up at you," I said.

And there we were. Me, a few inches taller than her, and the pair of us close enough to kiss. At this height I caught the fragrance of her favorite perfume, mingled with her natural warm body scent. The combination was ambrosia to me, bringing back the memory of the redolence of her sweat after our enthusiastic lovemaking.

"You're probably wondering why I came here," Jyanette said and turned from me, the closeness obviously a little too intimate for her as well.

"It crossed my mind."

"I wanted to apologize," Jyanette confessed.

I frowned. "You have nothing to apologize for."

"Yes, I do," she went on. "I ran out on you, without a thought as to what you were going through."

"Jyanette, you were injured, badly. You lost the baby—"

"I know," Jyanette murmured, and hung her head. "My doctor says that I can never have children."

I stood there helpless, as she began to cry.

I moved to her and put my left arm on her shoulder. "Leaving wasn't your fault, none of it. You needed to get away, needed to heal."

"But I haven't healed, Len," she lamented, still facing away from me.

"It's only been a few months. You have to give yourself a chance."

She turned to me, tears streaming down her face. "I miss you."

I thought I couldn't be any more stunned than when I'd seen her that morning. She moved into me and put her arms around me. I was sure I was dreaming, that this had to be a fantasy I'd somehow brought to life.

I put my left arm around her and held her, thrilled to have her there and saddened by her pain. For once, I had no idea what to say, or what to do, fearful of breaking this spell.

She broke it. She stepped over to a side table where I always kept a box of tissues, to dab her eyes and blow her nose.

As she parted from me, I spoke as well. "I've missed you, too. Terribly."

She finished wiping her eyes and threw the tissue away. "Well, we made choices—

"You leaving was not my choice," I told her.

She sighed and nodded her head. "All right, *I* made a choice, and now I have to live with it."

"Jyanette, you're here, I'm here. If you want to change things…"

"I can't, Len," she said, and began to button up her coat. "Dammit. I was an idiot to come here."

"Jyanette, I don't know what to say, or what I should say…" I attempted.

Her face grew stern as she finished closing the coat. "Do you know why you were called in on this case?"

"At the meeting, it seemed that the FBI was impressed by how we stopped Doctor Vanya."

She faced the door. "You're only on this case because I recommended you to Agent Calvin."

"Um… thank you?"

"He only agreed because… we're dating," she said, not looking back at me. As I stood in shock once again, she opened the door and stepped out into the night without another word.

I moved to the window and peered through the sheer curtains. She was getting into a car, not her own, but a large dark vehicle with government plates.

As she pulled open the passenger door, the light came on and I could see the driver.

Agent Calvin.

I collapsed into my wheelchair, my mind reeling.

Talk about mixed messages! On one hand, she missed me, on the other, she had been driven here by her new boyfriend.

A part of me was furious. How could she be dating? It hadn't been all that long.

Of course, the fact that I'd been having sex with Kate since Christmas didn't immediately cross my mind. Jyanette and I had not been intimate since June of the previous year, and that encounter had resulted in the unplanned pregnancy.

The child that had been unplanned, had certainly not been unwanted. When the horrific events of the previous September unfolded, Jyanette lost the baby and ended up in the hospital. She left New Jersey to move in with her parents and build a new life in the Washington DC area.

It was hardly surprising that such an attractive woman would be asked out, especially by the tall, and I had to admit, handsome FBI agent. Since she worked with the DOJ it was not surprising that they had met.

I tried to quell any feeling of jealousy toward Agent Calvin. After all, I was merely angry that he was with her, and I wasn't.

Any thought that she was *mine* was mere illusion. She wasn't mine or anyone else's, she was her own person, her own woman. Perhaps seeing each other again was as confusing to her as it was to me.

I moved to my phone and called Bill.

He answered on the first ring. "McGee."

"Lindwall and two of his men are holed up in an RV."

"*What?* Where?"

"I didn't get that."

"We'll put out the alert to start searching any RV parks in the area."

"I have a feeling that won't work. They were using an oil lamp for illumination, and there weren't any streetlights outside the vehicle."

"I see. If they were in an RV park they'd have hook ups for electric and water, and the area would be lit."

Things were so easy working with Bill, as his sharp mind filled in my unspoken connections. "Right. I think they're somewhere in the woods. I don't know how far from here, but I think they want to stay close to the area."

"Why do you think that?"

"Lindwall mentioned something about timers he needed to release the virus. He needs to pick them up once they arrive."

"Any idea when that will be?"

"I have to say a day or two at the most."

"I'll get this information to the Feds. Thanks, Len."

I ended the call, feeling totally exhausted. I was wrung out from physical therapy, my partially successful reading, and the emotional upheaval of the day. I went into the bathroom, brushed my teeth, and took the nighttime pain-killer that would help me sleep.

As I lay in bed waiting for the pill to knock me out, all I could see was Jyanette, and the overwhelming apprehension that I had lost her forever.

4. MENTAL INFIRMITY

I wheeled into the MPD at seven-fifty-five AM. I had forgone the pain pill this morning, taking an ibuprofen tablet instead so my abilities wouldn't be affected. I did manage to shave and dress in shirt, pants, and a suit jacket instead of sweats. I hoped I looked more professional today.

I was surprised to find a pair of large SWAT-style black step vans in the MPD parking lot, looking very militaristic. It reinforced the fact that this situation was being taken very seriously.

I was concerned about how I would react to Jyanette and Agent Calvin, but I need not have worried. The meeting started the moment I got into the room.

The room was more crowded today, with men in black uniforms, tactical vests, and side arms standing in the back. Besides Agents Calvin and Marsh, there were several other men in dark suits that suggested FBI. Gabe Petrie was on one side of the table with several of his team, as well as Kate.

McGee was at the end of the table, seated next to Captain Harris, the police chief of Mountainview. His dark face was creased with annoyance, as if the fact that this was happening in his town was a personal insult.

Calvin moved to the front of the room, the overhead lights reflecting off his shaved head. "Due to a tip given us by Lieutenant McGee last night, several recreational vehicles were located and searched in the Hawk Rock Reservation, as well as the South Mountain Reservation. They were all people with overnight passes and were legitimately staying at these locations."

"How did the Lieutenant receive this tip?" grumbled Petrie, and he held aloft a paper. "As well as the suggestion these terrorists are waiting for a shipment of some kind?"

McGee cleared his throat. "We have every available asset on this case. I was able to get some chatter from the streets. I think the information is reliable."

Gabe made a face, as if he'd tasted something unpleasant. "Didn't result in finding Lindwall or any of his crew."

"But it did give us a place to start." Marsh looked over at McGee. "We're talking to RV dealers in New Jersey, Pennsylvania, and New York, showing photos of Lindwall. If we can know the specific type of vehicle he purchased, we'll have a better chance to track him down."

"Provided he didn't get it used from an individual," Petrie complained. "Or have another member of the group buy the vehicle."

Captain Harris rose and spoke with his booming voice. "Gentlemen, what we are here to discuss today is the evacuation and lockdown of Mountainview. It may become necessary if this virus is indeed released."

Harris took over the meeting. Using a screen and laser pointer, he went over a very complicated plan that would be put into action if the virus were released. It included shutting down the trains and blockading the roads in and out of the town as far out as Bloomdale and West Orange.

The prospect was horrifying.

They also had more information from tests run on the dead lab animals and the results made everyone more nervous. Since I had the background, I understood this part even though my medical career had been focused on surgery and not immunology.

Dengue Fever is an infection caused by the dengue virus, usually through a mosquito bite, so the virus has to be injected into the blood stream. The results from the viral infection are damage to the lymph system and blood vessels.

However, by infecting the tuberculosis bacteria with the dengue virus, it allowed the virus to enter through the lungs, and directly into the circulatory system. This would lead to massive bleeding, shock, and death through what was known as 'dengue shock syndrome' in a matter of a few short hours.

From the autopsies of the lab animals, the lungs and circulatory systems were destroyed in all of the victims, and the virus had been harvested from the blood of the infected animals.

Questions flew about the room, with Marsh and Calvin taking the lead for the FBI response. Petrie brought up suggestions that were actually quite good. I was not a big fan of Gabe, but I knew he could run an operation successfully.

The only person who I felt was not up to this job was *me*.

These people were all professionals and some of the suggestions, though ruthless by my standards, might be necessary to avoid a terrorist attack from becoming a pandemic.

Hard choices would need to be made, since it meant that the possible loss of life in Mountainview could be staggering.

Finally, after two hours, Captain Harris called for a break.

I wheeled into the hall as the twenty or so men descended upon the canteen, seeking coffee and the vending machine with its limited supply of snack foods.

As I sat in the hall, my leg in pain from the surgery as well as from my PT the previous day, Kate leaned forward to speak to me.

"You don't look good, Len," she said softly.

"It's all a bit overwhelming. The results would be terrible."

"That's why we need to stop it. Do you mind if I push you into the computer room so we can talk?"

"Sure," I responded and pulled the handle to release the brake.

We went across the hall to the large computer room. Besides desks where computers and servers whirred and clicked, there was a large conference table in the center. This was the secondary conference room, and I had a feeling that we would have so many people joining us in the next few days that it would soon be filled as well.

One of the desks was set up for our resident computer expert, Ben Galland, the blond haired, blue-eyed officer who often acted as McGee's aide-de-camp. I was one of the few people who knew he was gay, as he'd been involved with my TA Teddy Santos. Even in this day and age Galland kept it hidden, due to the macho atmosphere that surrounds policemen and their work.

The room was empty and we were alone.

Kate got right to the point. "I'm guessing the tip about the RV and the bit about terrorists waiting for a shipment came to McGee through you."

"One could assume that," I conceded.

"No fix on the location?"

"I was focused on Lindwall, and the camper was only lit with an oil lamp."

"So, you saw him, in that special way of yours. Anyone with him?"

"Two men, one blond with a Southern drawl and another with a scar over his eye."

"I've got photos of the people suspected to be part of the Faction on a tablet. Perhaps you can identify them?"

I nodded. "That would be good, then I can feel like I'm helping, even if it's only a little."

"We need more than we have, but Petrie and Marsh don't have any idea how to work with you," Kate warned. "I could use hypnosis to help you achieve an alpha state, and regress back to the memory of the RV. I might even be able to inspire you to have a vision of the location again, if I help you focus."

"That's a good idea," I agreed. "I'm a bit distracted by my leg."

"You couldn't take the painkiller?"

"Opiates interfere with my readings."

"I think it makes more sense if you and I did some hypnosis, rather than sit in meetings talking about barricading roads."

I nodded. "I have to admit, I was feeling pretty useless in there."

"Will it bother your ex if I work with you?"

I looked up at Kate, trying not to fall into abject misery. "It won't. Turns out, she's dating Agent Calvin."

This made Kate's eyebrows go up. "Well, he *is* a good-looking man."

"Can we just focus on the mission?" I muttered.

Kate shook her head. "I guess they removed your sense of humor when they replaced your knee."

"Probably," I croaked as Kate left the room to clear us working together outside of the meeting.

I needed to get my head in the game. The visit the previous night from Jyanette had surprised me, then left me depressed. Why did she even visit me if she was dating another man? She said it was to apologize for running out on me, but she could have done that over the phone.

I had to let all of this go and try to locate Lindwall and his associates.

Kate came back with a tablet in her hand.

"Here are the photos of known associates. You look these over, while I figure out the best place to do this."

I took the tablet from her. "What's wrong with this room?"

She looked around. "They'll need this space soon. They're expecting the biohazard team from the Department of Homeland Security."

"I thought they were still running analysis at the warehouse?"

"Apparently they finished up, and one of them will be leading the afternoon session," Kate explained. "They'll need this room for the overflow. Besides, I want something smaller, and maybe a place I can turn off the lights, and you can lie down."

I raised an eyebrow. "Maybe one of the holding cells?"

"Oh sure, great place to relax," she scoffed.

"How about one of the bunk rooms? They each have a bed, and we can bring a chair for you."

She considered this. "Across from the locker room, right? I think that will do. And there's no need to bring in a chair. You can lie down, and I'll just sit in your wheelchair."

That made sense since I had to roll into the room anyway.

"Look over the photos, and I'll check the rooms, make sure there is one available."

"Get me one of the prints of those photos of Lindwall they were passing out last night," I said. When she glanced over with a puzzled look I added. "I need something tangible to focus on, the tablet isn't the same."

She left the room and I focused my attention on the tablet for now. The first photo was the posed one of Lindwall, and I used my index finger to scroll to the next one... and the next. After about the sixth photo, the face of the blond-haired man appeared on the screen. It was obviously a mug shot, taken from a different jurisdiction, but I recognized him easily. A number was listed under his face and the words: "South Orange Police."

"Okay, we're cleared," Kate said, as she came back into the room and handed me one of the 8x10s of Lindwall. "Bunk Room One is free."

I held out the tablet. "This is one of the men I saw."

She took the device and looked at the image, scrolling to get more information. "Godfrey Hermann."

"Godfrey?" I questioned.

She read the tablet as she spoke. "Yeah, calls himself 'God' for short. Born in Clanton, Alabama, which explains the Southern accent. Troubled childhood, parents divorced, petty crimes at a young age. Several restraining orders, as he apparently likes to beat up women, and has committed sexual assaults as well. Moved around the country a lot, suspected in a long list of crimes, including multiple hate-crimes."

"Sounds like someone Lindwall would want on his crew," I said as Kate handed me back the tablet and pushed my chair down the hall towards the bunk rooms.

I continued to go through the photos as we entered the room. These small spaces were not meant to be very welcoming, as their function was for a police officer to catch a few hours of shuteye between shifts when necessary.

It was a modest rectangular room with just enough space next to the single bed to fit my wheelchair. The walls were a dark blue, and a blackout shade covered a window that would be eye level if I were standing. The window was sealed, and far too small for anyone to crawl through even if the glass was removed.

I handed the tablet to Kate and used my cane to push myself to my feet before lying down in the bed. She handed me back the tablet with a coy grin on her face.

"What?" I asked.

"You know, if we locked the door…" she said with a lifted eyebrow.

"I'm not in the mood," I admonished. "Besides, we'd make too much noise."

"You have a point," Kate smiled. "Sometimes it sounds like I'm killing you."

"Can we focus on helping me achieve an alpha state, please?"

She stuck her lower lip out in a pout. "You used to be fun."

"I also didn't have a deadly virus ready to wipe out my town," I complained, sorry that I encouraged this at all.

"Okay, okay," she said and sat in my chair.

I had continued to go through the photos on the tablet as we spoke, keeping my attention on the device and only looking up occasionally, so as not to encourage Kate's carnal interest. I flipped through them, and there in front of me was the man with the scar on his forehead. It also appeared to be a mug shot and it showed a file number and "Fanwood Police Department" underneath the placard he held.

"This is the second man I saw." I held out the tablet for Kate.

"Ah, Derrick Johnson. Part-time bouncer, and bodyguard for a while. He's ex-military, with a dishonorable discharge. Then he started to get into bar fights and was locked up a few years back for killing a man."

"Another fine upstanding citizen," I quipped.

"Let me text Gabe that these two men might be with Lindwall. If we can get an APB out on them, we might catch one when they get supplies or something."

I lay back on the uncomfortable bed. Until I could take another painkiller, I couldn't get comfortable anywhere.

Kate used the touch-screen device and typed a quick message, as I held the printed photo of Lindwall.

"We also need to find someone named Tommy," I told her.

"Tommy?" Kate repeated, still typing. "They don't list anyone in the group with that name."

"Well, he's important to their plans."

Finally, she set the tablet aside. "In the meantime, let's move on to you."

"Make sure I remember the session," I demanded. "I don't want you creating any post-hypnotic suggestions."

"I don't know," Kate grinned. "Making you cluck like a chicken could be very entertaining."

I had to admit, that image made me smile as well. Why was I being so hard on Kate? Maybe she was just trying to lighten the mood. Pining over Jyanette was spoiling the good thing we had between us.

Sighing, I lay back and shut my eyes.

"Listen to the sound of my voice, nothing but my voice. You are relaxing, letting all tension go. Feel your feet relax…"

She went on with the simple hypnotic technique of mentally traveling up my body and relaxing each section: legs, hips, torso, etc.

By the time she reached my head I was in a very relaxed state, indeed.

From a distance I heard her speak. "There is a man you are looking for, Joseph Lindwall. Picture him clearly in your mind. Find him, find him where he is right now."

When I try to do a reading of anyone, it is helpful if I have some personal object to focus my efforts. I caressed the photo with my hand, almost like a talisman. I listened to her words and brought up my memory of Lindwall around the table of the vehicle the previous night.

In my mind, the vision shifted and I stood in front of the same table, but now it was bathed in sunlight as it streamed in through the covered windows of the RV.

At the table sat Lindwall, a mug in his hand, and I assumed he was having his morning coffee.

"I'm there," I whispered aloud.

"Where are you?" Kate asked.

"In the RV. I think he's there now, it's morning."

"Can you see outside the window?"

I shifted my eyes away from Lindwall and moved to one of the windows on the side of the vehicle to peer through the gap of the curtain. I could see skeletal tree branches outside and brown grass under small bushes. The camper appeared to be in a small parking lot as there was macadam directly outside the vehicle. It couldn't be a campsite, as the tiny parking space I was able to see couldn't hold more than a few vehicles.

"They're near the woods, in a small parking lot."

"At a campsite?"

"I'm... not sure."

"Are there any signs?" Kate asked. "Anything you can see to identify the location?"

I looked over the landscape, trying to find something that could give me a fix on the vehicle's whereabouts. All I could see out of this window was the winter forest on one side. I moved to the other bank of windows to peer through a small gap where I saw a small one-story building. It was little more than a shed, painted bright red with a white metal door. Several large white pipes rose out of the pavement and into the building. I assumed they carried electricity or plumbing into the structure. The pipes seemed overlarge to serve such a tiny building. If they were electrical, then a lot of power was going through the small shed.

I moved down the row of windows, and through the gaps in the curtains I could see out toward the end of the camper. There was a gray box, supported off the ground in a wooden frame, with hook-ups for electricity and water.

"Wait, it might be a campsite, there's a box for electricity."

"That would explain how they keep warm," Kate suggested.

I looked out the window further into the distance and could see a sign on a pair of posts. The sign was painted a bright brown as many informational signs are in New Jersey, but I couldn't see what was printed on it from the angle open to me. There was something blue and possibly a bird, but it was too far away to be sure.

The sign seemed familiar, but I couldn't figure out why. The configuration, even the color of brown was something I had seen before, but I didn't have the context to allow it to make sense.

I turned back to look at Lindwall as he sipped his coffee. He had a laptop open in front of him and was studying something intently.

I moved until I was behind him. In this astral state I don't really *walk*. I sort of glide over to where I want to be, moved by thought more than physical action since I wasn't in a physical body.

On his screen was a device, and the plans were showing how the different parts fit together to create an atomizer with a timer and how to attach it to a tank. The words on the page spoke of "Delayed Aerosol Release."

The door of the RV opened and a voice called up. "Is it safe?"

"I'm alone," Lindwall said, not looking up from his screen.

"Ah, the rover boys are gone?" she said, coming up the stairs. She stopped at the top of the steps and I was looking at one of the most beautiful women I had ever seen. She was tall and fit in tight jeans and a fur coat, and she was achingly *familiar*.

I had seen this woman before.

The oddest thing was that instead of looking at Lindwall, she was staring right at me.

She cocked her head, her eyes still on me. "Hello there. Who are you?"

I felt exposed, even though I knew this was impossible! I wasn't really there in the RV, I was in the bunk room at MPD. There was no way this woman could possibly be looking at me.

Yet she was.

At this point, even Lindwall was looking away from the computer and up at me but I thought he was just staring into empty space.

"What's up, Lanie?"

"Shh!" she hissed at Lindwall. She returned her eyes to me. "I think you'd better go."

I had the sensation of falling, falling down a long tunnel, and I sat up in the narrow bed, my eyes wide as I gasped for breath.

"Len!" Kate chirped, quite surprised. "That's a terrible way to come out of a trance."

"Water," I gasped, as I fought to slow my pounding heart.

"Okay, okay, but you need to lie back," Kate rose and exited the room.

I lay my head on the pillow and tried to get my brain around what had just happened. This woman had seen my ethereal body as if I had been standing there. When she told me to leave, I was thrown out and back into my physical body.

Suddenly all those Biblical stories of prophets casting out spirits made a whole lot more sense to me.

There was only one explanation.

This woman — this Lanie — was a psychic.

And she could do things that I couldn't.

5. SPIRITUAL AILMENT

"That's not possible," Kate said as I guzzled down the bottle of water she'd brought me.

I paused so I could answer. "She *saw* me! She was aware I was in the room. Don't you see how profound that is?"

"To be honest, not really. You've told me *you* can see ghosts."

"Yes, but they're disembodied spirits. I was only there mentally."

She touched my head. "Len, did you see anything that could point us to where Lindwall is?"

I paused for a moment and considered what she said. That had been the reason we had done this, to get a clue to Lindwall's whereabouts. The shock of being "cast out" had taken my attention from that fact.

"He was someplace with an electrical connection, I know that. And I saw a brown wooden sign, the kind the state puts in all the recreational areas."

Kate's eyes brightened. "Did you read what it said?"

"It was too far away. All I could see was that there were two words in white letters and a blue bird — like a goose or something."

"Close your eyes, lay back—"

"I'm not going to try to go there again—"

"Shh," Kate comforted me. "I don't want you to. I just want you to remember the sign."

I closed my eyes and allowed Kate to lead me.

"Now think back. You saw a sign."

I went back in my memory and saw the sign in the distance, past the small red building. "Yes."

"Bring it into focus. You said there were two words. Try to see them."

I frowned in concentration.

"Don't force it," Kate soothed. "Allow it to happen. Just let yourself see the sign."

I could see the wood, painted with the flat brown paint used for many recreational areas throughout the state. The blue goose seemed to come into tighter focus and I could see its outstretched wings. Next to it were white letters with the name of the location.

The letters started to come into focus.

I leapt up again, my eyes wide. "Great Swamp," I bellowed.

"Len, you must stop doing that!" Kate snapped. "It's very—"

"The Great Swamp," I insisted. "That's what the sign said."

I grew up in New Jersey, unlike Kate, and was familiar with the area known as the "Great Swamp." It was in nearby Morris County, and was designated as an untouched habitat.

Kate met my eyes. "Is there a lot of space to hide an RV?"

I considered this. "Thousands of acres, but I saw an electrical hookup. How many of those could they have there?"

"You stay here, I'll go get Bill," Kate said, rising.

"No, I can—" I began, but she was already out the door.

I got myself carefully up on my feet and into my wheelchair. My right leg ached and I hoped I had done enough so that I could go home and take a painkiller.

I got the door open and myself out to the hall, just as Kate walked up with Bill by her side.

"You've got something, Len?"

A part of me wanted to respond with, "Yeah, an aching leg and a headache," but I controlled myself.

"Yes, Bill. I think the RV we are searching for is somewhere in the Great Swamp."

"Jeez," he muttered. "That area is huge and there are several roads going in and out—"

"I know, but the RV is near one of those brown signs, and a small red building."

"A small red building?" Bill repeated and glanced over to Kate and then back to me. "In the Great Swamp?"

"Yes, and they have an electrical hookup as well. I have no explanation for it, but that's what I saw."

Bill nodded. "I'll get Galland to call over there and see if they have any place in the swamp that fits that criteria."

"Sorry it isn't more, Bill."

"It's something, which is more than we have so far," Bill said and headed down the hall to the computer room, looking for Galland.

Kate took my hand. "How do you feel?"

"Pretty wiped. I think I'm going to drive home, do my exercises, and take a nap."

"Doctor Yearling," Jyanette said, suddenly appearing in the outer doorway that led to the bunk rooms.

I snatched my hand away without thinking.

"You're needed in the meeting," Jyanette told her, obviously noticing my quick movement. "They want to go over your profile on Lindwall."

"Of course, Ms. Emery," Kate replied with a quick glance in my direction.

She walked past Jyanette who looked at me with a stony expression. She glanced at the open bunk room and then at me and crossed her arms. "Needed some rest?"

"We did a session of guided hypnosis. Kate was helping me to find Lindwall."

"Any luck?"

"Maybe. Bill is having Galland do some checking. I don't know if it will pan out."

She nodded. "I'd better get back in there."

"Thank you," I blurted, stopping her in her tracks.

She looked at me quizzically.

"For coming to my place last night, and… apologizing. I'm sure that was difficult for you."

She sighed. "You have no idea."

"I have to ask — why did you?"

Jyanette glanced back to the doorway where the meeting was going on. "Seeing you in the wheelchair. I don't know, it… bothered me."

"You used to complain that I kept getting hurt all the time."

"Yes, that always frightened me. But seeing you so… I don't know — vulnerable — I felt bad."

She stared at me in silence for a moment.

"I have to get back in," she finally said.

"Sure. I'll be… around."

She nodded and headed back to the meeting.

I suck at romance.

I should have said something, told her that not a day went by that I didn't long for her.

At least I hadn't started crying.

Despite what romance novels suggest about sensitive men, many women do not prefer men who shed tears over broken hearts. They might not go for a "macho" guy, but they also don't care for weepy ones.

I guess emotionally stable and secure is the middle ground. Jyanette left me because I was neither.

I had been in a lot of scrapes over the last two years, but I felt they were always for a good cause, helping other people, solving crimes. I'd had bumps and bruises and a few stitches. The only reason I was in a wheelchair now, was because of the operation I had by choice. The impact of my exploits had been far worse on Jyanette than on me.

After what happened to her, Jyanette could never have children.

That was a far more devastating injury, and one so profound, I knew I could never fully appreciate it.

I decided to get a cup of coffee while everyone was in the meeting, then go home to painkillers, exercises, and a soft bed. Let the professionals catch the bad guys for once.

I rolled down the hall. With almost everyone in the meeting, the hallways at MPD were empty of the usual bustle of people moving to and fro, criminals being booked, and the non-stop craziness of a police station.

I wheeled into the Canteen and started to brew my one cup of coffee. I sat there as it burbled and hissed, trying not to think of my painful knee or my broken heart.

If I had any sense, I'd call Kate and ask her to come over once she was done for the day. If I couldn't be happy, at least I could enjoy some physical attention. She had dropped enough hints, after all, so there was no doubt she was willing.

Just as my cup finished, Sergeant of Detectives Joseph Tice walked into the room.

When I'd met him, Tice and I had not hit it off, in fact he took every chance to berate me. Over the last two years, he had slowly developed a grudging respect for me, though he still called me "witch-doctor" and other colorful nicknames.

"It's the fortune-teller," Tice said. "Do they have you reading runes today?"

I had to admit, his words were much more playful than when we'd first met.

"Anything that helps," I said, grabbing my styrofoam cup. "Want me to start you a cup, Tice?"

"Yeah, sure, Doc. How's the leg?"

I put my cup on the counter and prepared the machine. "Hurts. I'm going to head home in a few minutes."

Tice frowned as the coffee brewed. "Aren't the painkillers any good?"

"I can't take them if I have to do any kind of reading."

Tice nodded. "Yeah, that's right. Drugs affect your mojo."

I nodded as the machine burbled and streamed out the hot brew. "I have to tell you, if I knew I'd be working a case, I'd have planned the surgery for a different time. Limping to a crime scene was bad enough, but rolling up in a wheelchair is worse."

"Yeah, but the chair is only for a couple of weeks, right?"

"I guess," I muttered.

I pulled Tice's cup and held it up for him. He took it and our eyes met.

Alaina...

I get flashes of precognition, which I call 'buzzes'. I don't know where they come from, but they have saved my life on occasion, and led me to find answers I could not have located through normal investigation techniques.

Now I was getting a strong one.

A memory appeared in my mind of a time when Tice thought I had committed a crime and had me in Interrogation. He made me so angry that I reached into his mind to pull up a memory that would hurt him.

What I did see in that brief moment was a young woman. She was breathtakingly beautiful and she looked into his eyes and said, "I'm sorry, Joseph, but I'm leaving."

At that moment, I felt his utter despair. That memory was so painful that any other man would have been crushed, but Tice carried on, did his duty, did his job, and at the time it filled me with wonder and pity. That moment of remembrance had been so very personal that I was embarrassed I had even glimpsed it.

The woman I'd seen in that short vision was the same woman who had cast me out with nothing more than a thought. She was older than in Tice's memory, but it had to be her. She was working with Lindwall as part of his team.

"You gonna let go, Doc?" Tice said, snapping me back to reality.

Tice took his coffee and sipped it, looking at me like I was insane. I'm sure that at that moment, I appeared crazed.

"You okay, Doc?" Tice worried.

"Do you know a woman named Lanie?" the question tumbled out of my mouth.

Tice's expression grew hard and I could see his back stiffen. "What?"

"A woman — maybe Alaina — called Lanie?"

His expression shifted, and I could now see fury in the man's eyes. "Did you get into my head?"

I could see I needed to diffuse the situation. "No. I... got the name, I think it's a woman named Lanie—"

Tice turned and carefully put down his coffee, then he slowly got on one knee in front of my chair and gripped the lapels of my suit jacket roughly in his hands.

"*Where* did you get that name?" he growled and I could feel his hot breath on my face.

"I had a vision, I saw her, talking with the terrorists—"

"Liar!" he bellowed. For a skinny guy, Tice had an iron grip and I thought he might pull me out of the wheelchair and throw me across the room.

I was saved by the booming voice of Bill McGee.

"Tice, what the hell are you doing?"

I looked over and saw my large friend in the doorway with a shocked expression on his face. In two strides, he was across the room and had his hand on Tice's shoulder.

Tice let me go and shrugged off McGee's hand as he stood. He glared up at McGee who was at least six inches taller than he was.

"Your boy got into my head," Tice snapped. "Thinks it's funny to play around." He glared back at me. "Some things aren't a joke, smart guy."

"It wasn't a joke," I explained, trying to explain what had just happened.

"What's this about?" Bill demanded.

"He thinks it's funny to bring up my ex-wife's name," Tice fumed. "He's trying to screw with my head."

"It wasn't like that at all. I got the name from a buzz."

"Oh yeah, you and your bullshit—" Tice spat.

"Tice, let's hear him out," Bill said, trying to calm him. "What's this about, Len?"

"Kate used hypnosis to get me to a lower level and try to track down Lindwall. But a weird thing happened. There was a woman with him. Lindwall called her Lanie."

"What's that got to do with Tice?"

Both men stared at me, and I had to come up with something. I guessed that the truth was the best thing I could do.

"One time, I… glimpsed a memory that Detective Tice had… of a woman…"

"This is bullshit—" Tice said.

"Let's hear him out," Bill soothed.

"The woman Tice remembered was the same woman. In the vision I just had, she was a little older, but it was her."

Tice turned his attention to Bill. "Is this the terrorist case you're working on?"

"Yeah. We didn't bring you in because someone had to handle the day-to-day cases, Tice."

Tice returned his focus to me. "Are you saying Lanie got mixed up with *terrorists*? You are truly full of shit, Wise."

"Calm down, Tice. Look, if there is even the smallest possibility that your ex is involved in this, we've got to look into it. Do you know how to get in touch with her?"

Tice looked between McGee and me as if he was watching a ping-pong match. "Only if you guys bring me in on the case."

"Tice, we've got the FBI, DOJ, and Homeland Security on this case. We need the rest of MPD to focus on other crimes, and you're the highest ranking detective—"

"That's the deal. If Lanie is involved, I gotta be in on it. I have to be in the loop."

McGee rubbed his head. "Tice, I'm not in charge, I can't—"

"Oh, you can't? Look Lieutenant, Lanie isn't someone I want to see, but I won't let her get railroaded over some tall tale the medicine man came up with."

"Okay, okay," McGee agreed. "You're in. Now about getting in touch with her—"

"Lieutenant, I found it." Officer Galland came into the small canteen.

McGee was not thrilled. "Found what, Galland?"

"The location in the Great Swamp. I spoke to one of the supervisors, and he said there's a RV hookup right across from their headquarters. And get this, there's a small utility building and it's painted red! I even found it on the street view on Google Maps."

McGee turned to me. "Do you think Lindwall's still there?"

I spoke up. "He could be, I only had the vision a little while ago."

Bill nodded, excitement in his eyes. "Galland, send the location to my phone, and I'll send it to the team."

"Yes, sir."

"Len, can you ride out too? You can still drive, right?"

I was tired and had no desire to go, but if it brought this to an end and stopped the madmen involved, it would be worth it.

"Yeah, I'm on it," I said.

"And I'm going with the shaman," Tice insisted, grabbing his coffee and taking a gulp.

"Okay, I've got to get a team ready to move out." Bill rushed out the door.

Tice looked down at me in my chair. He spoke in a threatening tone. "And you're going to explain how you got a memory of my ex-wife from me."

He left the room and I retrieved my own cup of coffee.

It was cold.

6. SITE CONTAMINATION

To say the ride out to the Great Swamp with Tice in my van was awkward would be an understatement. He glared at me without speaking, and I thought it best to not antagonize him.

He got himself up to speed on the situation by reading a folder McGee had slipped to him before he got into the passenger seat of my van.

Although late February and cold, the day was clear as we drove. I took highways for part of the journey, followed by small back roads through the towns of Gillette and Stirling.

The Great Swamp National Wildlife Refuge is seventy-five hundred acres of land in the middle of Northern New Jersey. It was formed tens of thousands of years ago, when retreating glaciers left a barren landscape and a large lake that eventually flows into the Passaic River. As the lake disappeared, the land became a series of marshes and swamps.

Towns were attempted in the area, but the wet land was not conducive for most crops, or construction.

Various modern uses were planned for the land: flood control in the 1920s, drainage projects in the 1930s, and even a major airport in 1959. But a small group, the North American Wildlife Foundation, raised more than a million dollars to purchase the acreage and donated it to the Department of the Interior. It was now a preserved recreational site, with the eastern half designated as a Wilderness Area.

On the positive side, there are only a limited number of roads in and out of the vast area, so it was possible to prevent escape in vehicles. On the negative side, someone with training in survival skills could move further into the swamp and hide from pursuit for weeks.

I tried to stay positive. The people we sought had an RV, which would be hard to conceal.

"Did you really see Alaina with this Lindwall guy?" Tice muttered to me.

I jumped a bit, as I had been lost in my own thoughts.

"Kate Yearling was using hypnotic techniques to help me focus, and I believe I saw her in a vision. Look, I could be wrong…"

"Damn straight," he grumbled. "And how did you, as you said, get a 'peek' into my memory?"

I took a deep breath. Trying to explain what happens to me is like trying to describe the taste of an apple to someone who has never eaten one.

I didn't want to tell him I had purposely invaded his mind to try to find something to hurt him with. It was one of the few times I had ever done that to anyone, and I still felt shame that I had attempted to use my abilities in such a base way.

"Look, Tice. My mind is constantly picking up the mental chatter of people around me," I attempted.

"Really?" he replied. His tone dripped with skepticism.

"It's like a constant background noise — and I have to work to shut it out. It's not just words or thoughts, but sometimes I get images, like if someone is really focused on something."

"So when did this 'glimpse' occur?"

"When you were questioning me about that incident with the female student."

At least that was true. A hypnotherapist had programmed one of my students to believe she had been sexually abused by me, and the girl was convinced it was true. I had been fortunate that there was a camera in my office that recorded the entire incident, and Bill and I were able to break the spell the young woman had been under.

Tice had been in on the arrest, and at the time, had been pretty rough on me.

Tice nodded. "Yeah, I remember thinking about Alaina that night, and was surprised the memory came back so strong. I can see how you might've picked up on it."

I nodded sagely, relieved that I didn't have to admit that I had pushed my way into his mind, but I didn't feel any less guilty.

"When I saw that memory, I didn't know she was your ex-wife. Not until you mentioned it today," I asserted. "And I got the name Alaina when I saw you."

"And where did *that* come from?" he demanded.

"I don't know. These 'buzzes' I get are little hints that just seem to come to me. My mentor, Doctor Kohl, believes that I can pick up the intentions of other people when they are focused on me. I get these random bits of information at the oddest times, and it seems like there is no rhyme or reason."

He returned his attention to the paper in the folder, falling into silence as I continued to drive.

Finally, without looking at me he said, "These things just pop into your head?"

"Pretty much."

"And you get thoughts and images from people around you, without wanting to?"

"If I don't focus to shut them out."

He glanced over at me. "That must suck."

"Yeah," I replied. "And the weird thing is that when I was a kid, I was perfectly normal. No visions or buzzes or anything."

Tice nodded. "McGee told me that this only started happening to you after the car accident where your fiancée died."

It was actually minutes before the crash, when I saw an eight-foot tall demon standing in the middle of the road, but I didn't think that would help my case.

Instead, I moved on from his premise. "When my abilities first started to manifest, I thought I was insane. So I went to California and enrolled in a psychiatry fellowship. It was there I met Doctor Kohl and he trained me in the use of my so-called gifts."

He lost interest in the papers and stared at the road ahead of us instead. "You really think Alaina is with this guy?"

"Tice, I couldn't tell you if she's dating him or just selling products door to door. I only caught a glimpse of her for a moment. What's more, a vision isn't evidence. I am just hoping it gave us a place to look."

He nodded slowly. "You know, she believed in all this stuff."

I frowned. "Your ex-wife?"

"Yeah," he said and the bitterness in his voice was obvious. "Back when we were married, she had this little altar set up in a closet of the spare bedroom. Used to do all kinds of things to 'raise her energy'."

I was listening intently now. Maybe he could give me a clue as to how she did the "cast-out" thing to me.

"I guess she took it pretty seriously, huh?"

Tice's lips moved back in what looked like a snarl. "She joined a fuckin' coven. I guess you know about that kind of stuff?"

"I studied it when I was doing my parapsychology degree. Nowadays, covens are mostly people who get together and practice pagan rituals."

"Yeah, well it killed our marriage. She got on this kick where she felt I was holding her back from her true power. That kind of crap."

This was a moment of epiphany for me. When McGee had first brought me into a case, he claimed I was a forensic pathologist, but even then, Tice and I did not get along. As time went on, it became clear to most of the detectives that I was McGee's 'pet psychic'. However, since we were closing cases at an unprecedented rate, most people didn't care how I did it, as long as it worked.

Tice, however, became even more hostile once my true role had been revealed. Now it all made sense. It wasn't me, per se, but the history of the metaphysical situations that had ruined his marriage.

No wonder he had resented me. I represented everything that had gone wrong with his marriage.

It was odd. I now looked at Tice in an entirely new way, and I wasn't sure I wanted to. It was just easier to dislike him, even with the uneasy truce that we had developed over the last few months.

We drove in silence for a few moments before approaching a pair of stone pillars that supported a fence that could be closed to block the roadway. The road was obstructed by a police car with its lights flashing. It bore an inverted triangle logo and the words "State Trooper" in letters on the side of the vehicle, signifying that this was a state officer, and not just local police.

"I'll take care of this, you stay here," Tice said, and stepped out of the van, showing his hands and talking to the trooper who stood outside his car. I watched as Tice approached, then pulled out his shield and ID which he handed to the trooper.

He and Tice talked for a minute, and Tice gestured at me in the van.

The trooper got into his vehicle and pulled it out of the way, and Tice got back in.

"The SWAT team and police cars just went by. They made better time than we did."

"You know I don't have sirens or flashing lights in this van, right?"

"And I doubt you ever will," Tice countered. "Let's see if they caught our guy."

We continued down the road, passing a small brown sign that read:

Great Swamp National Wildlife Refuge
Open sunrise to sundown

The trees that lined the road were skeletal except for the occasional pine, and the grass on the shoulders was brown. Up ahead, I could make out a SWAT van and several MPD police cars. I assumed that the FBI team had ridden with one group or the other.

I pulled the van into the lot, and then I saw it; the small red building I had glimpsed in my vision. It had a white door with a pane of glass in it. I shifted my gaze to the small parking lot to see the electric hookup I had also witnessed.

What was missing was the vehicle itself.

Several men in black tactical gear and armored vests that read HOMELAND SECURITY were milling about the red building as well as the small parking lot. They all carried automatic weapons hanging from harnesses on their shoulders.

When I pulled to a stop, Tice exited the van and made his way over to McGee who was speaking with Agents Petrie, Calvin, and Marsh.

I worked to get my wheelchair out of the van and used the lift to get to the ground. By the time I had wheeled my way to them, they were in a heated discussion.

"If they *were* here, how did they leave so fast?" Marsh complained.

McGee remained calm and professional. "Officer Galland went to the headquarters and spoke to the supervisor in person. The supervisor said he saw an RV on the road right after Galland spoke to him on the phone."

"There is no way they could have known we were coming," Calvin declared. "Are you sure your source was accurate on this?"

McGee held up a hand. "Hold on a moment." He moved away from the group and toward me. Without a word he grabbed my chair and began to push me toward the small lot where the RV must have been. "Can you tell me anything?"

"No, but if you can move me to the electric hookup, I might be able to get something."

"You mean besides electrocution?" he quipped, as he guided my chair in the correct direction. "Why do that Len, when there are so many people who would be willing to do it to you?"

"Fortunately, they're not here. If Lindwall left, I imagine it was in a hurry, the last thing he touched would be the hookups. I'm hoping I can get some clue as to where he went."

"How did they know to leave so quickly? I mean, it was less than an hour ago that you told me about it."

I turned my head and spoke so only Bill could hear. "It was the woman."

"What about her?"

"When I was in the RV, she could see me."

Bill frowned. "*See* you? See *what*? You were only there in your mind, right?"

"Yes and no. I used astral projection, but this woman could see me."

"Like you were a ghost?"

"That would be the easiest way to explain it."

"How could she see you? And then know to run?"

"I don't have answers for that."

At this point Bill had moved me about a foot away from the electric box. "Okay, I have to get back to the FBI. Calvin thinks he can get me a satellite view of this area from earlier this morning."

"He can do that?"

"Apparently so," Bill said as he stepped away.

"Big Brother really is watching."

Bill shrugged, then walked toward the other three men.

I looked at the electric hookup. It was a simple metal box attached to a wooden board, about two feet off the ground. A pair of metal conduits came out of the ground and into the box, which supplied the electric power.

I tapped the box once, just to make sure it wasn't electrified. Then I rested my right hand on it and closed my eyes, picturing Lindwall in my mind.

What is that guy in the wheelchair doing...

That weird guy is with the cops? I don't see what he does...

I just want an easy assignment for once...

I was picking up on the minds around me. The cops were all looking around and seeking any threats. The hardest to block were people who were looking and thinking directly about me.

I took a deep breath and focused on Lindwall, on the cold metal beneath my winter gloves, and trying to see who took down the hookups.

I saw a gloved hand, the fabric in a camouflage design.

The hand pulled a heavy wire with a plug loose and began to wrap it.

I saw Lindwall moving toward the RV, coiling the wire as he went. Next to the large RV was a small car, a simple bright green hatchback. I don't know cars, so I didn't recognize the make or model. In fact, if it weren't for the green color, it was entirely innocuous.

Lindwall stowed the rolled wire into a small open door on the base of the vehicle, slammed it down, and looked up.

Lanie stood in the doorway of the RV, watching him, her coat pulled tight.

"You really think he's gonna find us?" Lindwall asked in his gruff voice.

Lanie smiled. "Have I steered you wrong so far? Trust me, we have to go, and go *now*."

"Okay, I'm ready. I'll let the others know to meet at checkpoint B."

He strode into the RV but I couldn't follow. I was there looking at Lanie, who glared over at the electrical box, her mouth a tight line.

She stepped out of the RV and headed for her car as the motor of the larger vehicle roared to life.

"Doctor Wise," a voice said, and the image left me.

I opened my eyes to Agent Calvin. He was in a long dark coat, gloves, and a hat, which was probably a good choice in February since he had a shaved head.

"Yes, Agent Calvin."

I wanted to really hate this guy, after all, he was dating my ex. What was worse, I was sure Jyanette told him all about last night, as he was the one who drove her to my house. It's really humiliating to have the new guy hear stories about the ex-boyfriend, especially since I'd pretty much poured my heart out to her.

"Lieutenant McGee asked me to show you this," he said and held out a tablet. On the screen was an aerial shot of this lot. It showed the small building and a large RV parked beside it.

"This was taken at 8:30 this morning. So, an RV was definitely here." He took back the tablet. "Not that we know, for a fact, that it was Lindwall—"

"Of course," I agreed. I knew it for a fact, but I could understand him hedging his bets.

"We're going to see if we can track him from traffic cams," he stated flatly.

"There are traffic cams out here?"

"We're working on that. Lieutenant McGee says you're the one who led us here."

"I only found out that Lindwall might be near the Great Swamp. It was really McGee and Officer Galland who tracked down the building and this location."

He looked down at me in my chair. I'm used to standing at my six-foot-four height, which allows me to tower over most people. To be on the receiving end of someone looking down at me was intimidating.

"You want to tell me how you got this information?"

"I'm sure OGC Emery has explained what it is I do."

Probably in bed.

And that's when anger suddenly burst upon me, so unexpectedly, that I almost lost my breath.

This guy was sleeping with my girl.

"I've heard some reports, a lot of them pretty far-fetched if you ask me."

I wanted to yell at the man, insult him, even fight him, which would have been comical with me in the wheelchair and him a sturdy fellow with hand-to-hand combat training. My jaw was clenched. I was surprised he couldn't hear me grind my teeth.

"I didn't ask you, Agent Calvin, you asked me. Are we done?"

"I may want to speak to you later," he said as he turned to go.

I watched him move toward the other agents, and I sat there fuming.

It made no sense to hate him because he was dating my girl.

The truth was she *wasn't* my girl.

Not anymore.

All at once, I was a pathetic little man in a wheelchair who desperately wanted to go home, take a painkiller, and be left alone to wallow in his misery.

7. EVIDENT COMPLAINT

Tice went with McGee for the drive back, so I was left to head home by myself. I'd had enough for one day and couldn't see how I could do any more. The ache in my leg had grown steadily worse and I just needed to take a few hours off and try to nap. If I could help later, I would.

The timing on this could not have been worse for me. The surgery and recovery was all I had planned to do, with maybe a few classes. To be pulled into an emergency while still on the mend was just too much at once. Then add to that the emotional upheaval of seeing Jyanette…

I had been able to track Lindwall down and we would have had him if it hadn't been for this woman, this Lanie. Although I thought she looked exactly like Tice's ex-wife, I had no proof. Personally, I couldn't see how I could get *any* proof of who she was. If she was a psychic and aware of when people were closing in on Lindwall, she had an obvious advantage.

Also, we were not going after a mugger or a second-story man, but a paramilitary group with training, guns, and a virus they could release.

Since I was gunless, clueless, and in a wheelchair, I was both figuratively and literally outgunned.

This might have to be an investigation left to the big boys. After all, I was merely a consultant who occasionally collected a reward. I wasn't in fighting shape right now.

I went in the door at my end of the house and had no desire to go see Mrs. Higgins. I just wanted to lie down and try to forget everything for a few hours, but as soon as the outer door closed there was a gentle rapping on the sitting room door.

I sighed. "Come in?"

Mrs. Higgins walked through the door pushing a trolley that had a steaming bowl of stew and bread, as well as a glass of water and two Ibuprofen.

"What's all this?" I asked.

"Are ye gonna tell me ye had something to eat, when *ye* know that *I* know that ye would be lyin'?"

I grinned as best as I could. "Thanks Mrs. Higgins. I'm just not hungry—"

"They'll be none of that! Ye'll eat it and then ye'll lie yerself down for a nap, ye hear me, Doctor?" She waved the soup spoon at me, almost as a weapon. "Don' make me call yer mother, and have her come down here and box yer ears."

At this point I had no choice but to chuckle. "All right, I'll eat."

She put the stew and the bread out on my desk.

"Is this your bedside manner, intimidating your patients?" I asked.

"It's easier with a patient who listens, which is always the hard part with ye, Doctor."

I could smell the stew from where it sat and I had to admit, the delicious aroma made me hungry. I noted the Ibuprofen as she placed the pair of pills next to the bowl. "I don't need those, I'm going to take a painkiller."

"It moight be wiser to take these, Doctor," Mrs. Higgins explained. "You need to keep yer wits about ye."

"The painkillers don't make me dopey," I clarified.

"But they do affect ye, don't they?"

"They shut off my psychic abilities, but to be honest, I could use a little quiet right now."

"Take these and have a lie down. Ye'll feel better if you sleep a bit."

Without another word, Mrs. Higgins left the room, leaving my food and the trolley.

Mrs. Higgins has her own psychic insights, that she refers to as 'her wooman's intooition', that often came through at the most unexpected times.

I would be foolish to ignore it.

I took the Ibuprofen and then started to eat the chicken stew. It was filled with chunks of potatoes and root vegetables, spiced to flavorful perfection without being overdone.

I ate it all and had the bread, a hearty pumpernickel that was the ideal complement. It was obvious why Mrs. Higgins had cooked for several very well-to-do families over the years. Everything she made was delicious.

I rolled out of the office and into the bedroom just as my phone rang.

It was Bill.

"Yeah, Bill?" I said.

"I thought you were coming back here," he announced in his deep voice.

"Sorry, Bill, I need some rest. I'm still recovering and I tire easily."

"I understand, Len. It's just that we're on the clock here."

"I thought the FBI was going to track the RV with traffic cams or satellites or — hell — carrier pigeons for all I know."

"They're trying, but they're not having much luck. Those back roads don't have cameras and Lindwall is too smart to drive through any of the towns."

I sighed. "It's safe to say he's planned this out pretty well."

"Once he gets this delivery you say he's waiting for, will they be ready to release the virus?"

"I think so," I worried. "Any luck with this Lanie?" I had told Bill about her green car after I had my vision at the site.

"It would help if you had a license plate number for the car or the RV. Looking for a bright green car isn't much to go on."

"Is Tice looking into his ex-wife?"

"He's given me the last address he had, and I'm trying to track her down."

"That's a big step."

"He wasn't happy about it, but he knew we had to go after any lead we had. Her full name is Alaina Woods, and her background is Romani—"

"Romani?" I repeated.

"Yeah, we used to call them 'Gypsies,' but that word has a lot of negative stereotyping these days."

The woman I'd seen was of Romani descent. This could explain her knowledge of the use of psychic abilities. The Romani people are well known for having seers and fortune-tellers in their midst.

"I'm going to nap, but I'll come by the station later."

"The portable lab will be here, with all of the staff for it. MPD will be pretty crowded."

I took the hint. "I'll call you when I'm awake and if I get anything."

"I'll let you know what we find out about Ms. Woods."

I ended the call. I really was pretty useless to Bill right now. I could go and sit in the meetings, but to what end? My information doesn't come to me from meetings, and seeing Jyanette would just depress me.

I thought of the previous night, and her coming in the door. She looked so beautiful, and the moment when she said she missed me made my heart soar.

It was all just to say goodbye.

She was dating someone new, and I was just some old business that had to be cleared up, so her conscience could rest easy.

I pulled off my shoes, used my cane to stand, and fought to get my suit jacket off. I lay down on top of the bed fully dressed. I had a special pillow I put under my new knee when I slept, and I slipped it in place. My leg still hurt and I lay there wondering why I'd let Mrs. Higgins convince me not to take the painkiller I wanted so badly.

I closed my eyes and tried to relax.

Just who are you…

The words came into my brain completely unexpectedly. I focused my mind to try and locate the source.

Hello…?

How are you doing this…?

The voice in my head definitely sounded feminine. I decided to try the direct approach.

Lanie?

No response.

Lanie, you are involved with some bad people…

I could feel her out there, somewhere. I seemed to sense that she was in meditation and had been looking for me.

I decided to play my only big gun.

Lanie, Joseph Tice is worried about you…

I wanted to picture Tice in my mind from when we had been speaking in my van. But the image that came was Tice the time I had pushed my way into his mind, and the beautiful Alaina was telling him she was leaving.

You can't know that! That was private…

This thought came into my head with a vehemence that surprised me.

We know who you are, Alaina Woods. The police are after you now…

It's not what it looks like…

Lindwall wants to kill millions. He must be stopped…

I cannot explain. You must trust me…

I will stop you…

We shall see…

The banging on my side door startled me out of my nap, mental conversation, or whatever it was that I was doing. I sat up, cursing. I had not been able to get a fix on any kind of location. In fact, no images came to me while we were communicating.

The knocking occurred again, and I called out, "Coming!"

I then pulled myself into my wheelchair and rolled to the door.

I opened it to Agent Calvin.

"Doctor Wise," he said. "Is now a good time to finish our discussion?"

I didn't think for one minute that he cared if it was a good time or not. I wanted to be nasty and complain that I had been sleeping, or tracking down the bad guys, but I saw no point in that.

"Sure, come on in," I replied dully.

I wheeled out of the way and he came in and shut the door, as I went to my desk and booted up my laptop computer.

"I asked you earlier how you had found out about that location in the Great Swamp. Do you want to add to your testimony, now?"

"Testimony?" I asked, surprised he chose that word. "I have nothing to add. I got a lead and McGee and Galland were able to track it down. That's all."

He pulled out a thin notebook from his long, black winter coat. "Now you've asked McGee to search for a green car and a woman, Alaina Woods?"

"Yes."

"Once again, how did you get this information?"

"Agent Calvin, as I told you before, I am sure that OGC Emery explained what I do."

"Ms. Emery only told me that you were some kind of amateur profiler who's had a lot of luck in other cases. She suggested things 'come to you' in ways most people can't achieve."

I considered this. If you came right down to it, that did pretty much explain my abilities in a way that most people could accept.

Calvin went on, "I have to tell you, Doctor, I only accepted you as part of the team on Ms. Emery's recommendation. Also, I wanted to meet you."

This got my attention.

"Meet me?"

"Did Ms. Emery tell you that we're dating?"

I exhaled heavily and pushed down my anger. I didn't like where this was going. "She mentioned it."

"I wanted to see why she wanted you on this case, considering you pretty much ruined her life."

We stared at each other, and through a force of will, I slowly got to my feet and clutched my cobra-headed cane in my hand.

I rose to my full six-foot-four height, which put me well over his five-eleven. I now looked down at him. "You want to tread carefully here, Agent."

A small smile was on his face. "You gonna try to take me? Because I think standing up took all you had."

"No, I'm not going to *take* you. But what happened between Jyanette and myself is private. If she tells you, that's her business. But you don't get the right to talk to me about things you know nothing about."

"Fair enough," he said with a nod.

Calvin turned away from me and I put my cane under my right hand and shifted the weight off my aching leg, which now was screaming in pain.

Without looking at me, he asked, "Doctor, do you have any connections to white-supremacist organizations?"

"What?" I said, taken aback.

He glanced over his shoulder back at me. "I think the question is obvious."

I frowned. "Agent Calvin, I'm a Jewish man who used to date an African-American woman. I don't think such people would wish to have me as a candidate."

"Still, there is this uncanny ability to know where they were. And someone had to let Lindwall know it was time to leave." He turned to face me and sat on the corner of my desk. "That is, if he even had been in that location."

"The satellite photo displayed an RV," I pointed out. "You showed me that yourself."

"Which still doesn't prove that Lindwall was there. I have no way of verifying any of your data was correct."

"Look, Agent, you can act on my insights or you can ignore them. I was asked to be part of this investigation, but, personally, I'd rather be in bed. So, if there is nothing else…"

He looked at the floor. "It seems like Jyanette still has feelings for you."

My breath caught in my throat. Did she? Was it too much to hope that the woman I adored still loved me?

"I don't want you taking advantage of that," he declared.

"Once again, that is none of your business, Agent."

He rose and moved to the outer door. "I might make it my business, Doctor."

He opened the door and stepped out into the cold, clear afternoon. As soon as the door closed, I flopped into my wheelchair and rubbed my hurting leg, being careful of the stitches.

Just what I needed, another conflict!

I didn't know what to do. My momentary vision of Lanie had given me no helpful information regarding Lindwall's whereabouts and now I was angry at being bothered by Calvin, but elated at the thought that Jyanette still felt something for me.

There were enough confused feelings rushing through me to make my head explode.

I was pulled back to reality by my phone ringing. I had to wheel back into the bedroom to get it, and saw from the screen it was Kate Yearling.

"Hey, Kate," I offered as I hit the button.

"Hey, yourself. Where are you? Everyone came back and you weren't with them."

"I hit a dead end, so I went home. Really, Kate, I've been pretty useless on this entire investigation."

"Well, it's about to heat up. They caught Derrick Johnson."

"Who?"

"One of Lindwall's men, the guy with the scar on his head. The FBI got a hit from the APB, and he was picked up buying supplies at a supermarket, if you can believe it. McGee wants you to sit in on the interrogation."

8. DISEASED REASONING

I was on my way to MPD in less than twenty minutes. This capture was a breakthrough. I might be able to reach into this guy's mind and find the place Lindwall had mentioned, 'Checkpoint B.' Of course, Lindwall and his crew used codenames for everything. It made them sound more militaristic and revealed no useful information if they were overheard.

Arriving at the police station, the SWAT vans were now flanked by two enormous trailers that worked as mobile labs. One of these large portable facilities was connected to a semi-truck, the other stood untethered and I wondered how it had been brought there. The trailers were long, longer than a truck used for shipping, with thick heavy cables snaking out to supply them with electricity.

I did the arduous get-out-of-the-van-and-into-the-wheelchair dance, and soon rolled through the back door of MPD to find Kate or McGee.

To say the place was busy was an understatement. There were people in the hallways, some clad in black and some in white lab coats, all of them talking. I had to keep asking people to let me by, as there was little space to get my wheelchair down the hall.

Kate was in an intense discussion with Gabe Petrie and glanced over to see me battling to get through the hallway. She took over, loudly moving people and getting behind me to push my chair through the crowd.

The door to the computer room was open and I caught a peek of Jyanette talking to Agent Calvin. They were speaking in low tones and looking at a table, their heads close together.

Seeing them working together so closely was tough, especially after my visit from the stalwart FBI agent, but I needed to push past any of my longings or resentments and stick to the task at hand.

Instead of wheeling me to the interrogation room, Kate pushed the chair into the holding area, where the three cells for MPD's limited lockup were located.

Only one cell was filled.

I recognized the man from my previous vision, with the telltale scar on his forehead. Derrick Johnson looked up at me like I was a worm to be ignored.

Kate lowered her head and whispered in my ear. "This is the only place we can get some privacy."

"It will do," I said.

"I'll get McGee."

"Give me a few minutes alone, okay?"

She rose, nodded, and left me there.

I watched Johnson carefully. If I could just get him to make eye contact it would give me enough to slip into his mind. Then I might get a clue about where Lindwall was hiding and what the plan was for releasing the virus.

I attempted to get his attention. "I guess they found you, in spite of trying to hide out in the Great Swamp."

His eyes stayed on the floor. "What? They got cripples for cops now? Have to say, you don't look much like a cop."

"I'm also Jewish, so I guess I'm just here to piss you off."

"You look more like a lawyer than a cop," he said with a grunt.

"We found the location at the utility shed, and we know Lindwall is working with Lanie."

This got a raised eyebrow, but he still didn't meet my eyes.

"That lady's been useful. She helps Lindwall let off some steam, you know? Hey, you ain't the guy she was married to, are ya?"

"I didn't have that particular honor," I replied.

"She said he was a skinny cop, and you're skinny. Didn't say he was a Kike, though."

To punctuate the ethnic slur he raised his eyes to mine, almost as a challenge. I met his eyes and pushed my way into his head.

His eyes widened as he experienced my consciousness slipping into his own. I've had this done to me as well, and it is certainly an odd feeling. You feel exposed and surprised, you want to look away, break contact, but at the same time you feel riveted to the spot.

Where is Checkpoint B...?

Images flooded into my mind: somewhere in a forest, trees and green leaves, then again with autumn colors on the same trees. I struggled to see something that would give me context, any slight clue that could show me where it was.

Then all at once, I felt resistance and abruptly — I was out — as Johnson moved away from the front of the cell and shut his eyes.

"No, you don't," Johnson said, his eyes tightly closed. "Lanie told us all about this stuff some people can do. I'm not some weak-minded wetback or dumbass black fool. You can't pull that shit on me."

I remained in my chair and tried to recover. Johnson's sudden severing of my probe was an unexpected shock.

As Johnson turned his back to me, Kate and McGee walked in, followed by Jyanette.

"Where's my lawyer?" Johnson demanded, speaking over his shoulder. "I got rights."

"What you have are a bunch of charges against you, Mister Johnson," Jyanette countered. "However, if you cooperate, maybe you won't spend the rest of your life locked away in a prison for terrorists."

McGee interrupted. "And in case you didn't know, if that virus is released here, and you're stuck in that cell, you'll be one of the first to die."

Johnson raised his eyes to look at McGee. "We're willing to die for our cause."

"Dying from Dengue Shock Syndrome is a pretty nasty way to go," Jyanette stated.

"Any way is a good way," Johnson said. "Besides, I'm *white*. I got strong genes. It's you pickaninnies that should worry."

Suddenly, I was standing. Not sure how I managed it, but my rage had propelled me to my feet.

Jyanette, surprised by my quick movement, stepped in. "Doctor Wise, don't you have somewhere else to be?"

I looked at Jyanette as I got my temper in check. She had her 'lawyer face' on, and I have to admit I wouldn't stand a chance in a poker game looking for her to reveal her 'tell'.

I lowered myself to my chair, and Johnson glanced at me, but avoided my eyes. "Seems to have hit a nerve. I guess Hymie has a thing for blacks."

I wheeled out of the room, fuming, as Johnson continued to demand his lawyer, and Jyanette negotiated for his cooperation.

Back in the crowded hall, McGee stepped behind me and bent down near my ear. "Any luck?"

"He's had practice in how to resist mental probing," I snapped.

"Easy, don't take it out on me," Bill urged.

"Sorry," I said, calming down. "To have Jyanette have to deal with that... that... *animal.*"

I had to speak loudly over the sound in the hall from all the people talking.

Bill just shook his head. "Len, Jyanette has been dealing with situations like this for years. What do you think she did at the DA's office?"

Then and there, it struck me. I had never seen Jyanette in court, never sat in on negotiations with her. In fact, I didn't really have any idea what she did as a prosecutor.

Suddenly I felt ashamed. Here was a woman I knew, professed to love, and yet, I didn't have any appreciation about the garbage she dealt with on a daily basis. No wonder she took a job with the

DOJ. Today was probably the first time she'd had to deal with a scumbag in months.

Here I was, the great Doctor Wise, able to read minds and track down criminals because I could pluck clues out of the ether. Meanwhile, she had to go to court and deal with people like Johnson, who hated her for her job and the color of her skin.

My eyes stung and I rubbed them with the palm of my hand.

"You okay, Len?" McGee consoled. "Your leg probably is killing you."

"Yeah, something like that," I gasped.

Jyanette joined us in the hall. "Any luck getting his lawyer?"

"I called the number he gave us. The lawyer said he doesn't represent him, and that he's our problem," McGee explained.

"Another ethical lawyer," Jyanette sighed. "Did you call for a public defender?"

"I sent Galland to pick one up."

Jyanette nodded. "That might be one way to get them here quickly."

"National emergency," Bill said and then glanced at the pair of us. "I have to get back to—"

"Go on," Jyanette said, with a grin.

It was good to see her smile, even that little bit.

She stared down at me, all business. "I don't need you to defend me, Len."

I shook my head. "Sorry... I didn't plan it... it's just when he spoke to you that way..."

"You went all macho and had to defend the lady?"

I looked up into those brown eyes that still held my heart, and then had to look away.

"Look, Len," Jyanette said patiently. "I've dealt with racist scum like him before—"

"I know, I know."

"No, you don't know. It was part of my job, and one of the reasons I had to get away from it. There were just too many negative things in my life."

"Was I one of them?" I asked.

"Not all the time," she said, and turned to head back to the meeting room.

Kate approached. Apparently, she'd been watching us the entire time.

"Well, that was touching," Kate said, her eyes following Jyanette retreating through the crowd.

"Not a good time, Kate," I chided.

"No, I guess not," Kate murmured, and patted my shoulder. "I guess our good time is over, isn't it?"

Before I could respond, she followed Jyanette toward the meeting room. At this point, most of the people milling in the hall were moving into the conference room and the computer room, which held the overflow.

The hallway was emptying as I sat there, the pain in my heart much worse than the one in my leg. There was nothing I could do, *nothing* I could say that would fix this, either with Kate or Jyanette.

I felt helpless... and I didn't like it.

I wheeled my way back into the holding cells, where Johnson was sitting on the bed.

He smirked at me and taunted, "You back, Jew boy? Thought you'd be following the black whore."

He shifted his eyes to mine for only a moment, but that was all I needed.

My rage filled me, and I used it to push my way into his mind so hard and so strong, he was unable to shut me out or resist me.

Images flashed through our minds.

I saw a huge church with a sign that read "International Church of Christ." Then I saw several quick images: a trailer park with a plastic orange dragon on the front lawn; streets of houses converted from trailers into permanent homes on tiny lots; several large RV's hooked up to electric and water.

Finally, I saw a house among the trees, a building covered with brown wooden shingles that looked very old. Behind it was a cleared path that led into deep woods, hidden from the road by the building.

I yanked myself out, and Johnson shook his head and moved away from me deeper into the cell.

"You can't do that shit," he yelled at me. "That's an illegal search. You ain't allowed to look in my head."

"Aw, suck it," I answered and wheeled my way out.

In the empty hallway, I pulled out my smart phone and went to the maps app to input "International Church of Christ".

Just my luck that about a hundred dots appeared on the map, in locations that spanned from New York to Washington DC. I expanded the map focusing in on New Jersey, and this specific part of the state.

It turned out that there was one such location next to a golf club in Morris County. The golf course wasn't unexpected as there were dozens of such clubs throughout the state. I could see on the map that there was a huge area listed as the "Great Piece Meadows," that extended from Wayne to Fairfield. It appeared to take up a lot of land. It also had very few roadways that went either in or out of it.

As I explored the map a bit more, I discovered there was a trailer park just south of the church. I wondered if it had an orange dragon in front, like I had seen in the images I'd pulled from Johnson's head.

I then moved to the nj.gov website about the Preserve, and learned that it took up eleven hundred acres. New Jersey has a lot of preserved land up and down the state.

I had a hunch that if Lindwall was hidden in that Preserve, he got there through a little-known roadway behind an old farmhouse.

Now I had to think of a way to persuade the FBI where to start looking.

It would help if I had a better idea myself.

9. SITUATION INFLAMMATION

The troops of men and women were now sequestered in the conference room and the computer room, going over whatever contingency plan the FBI had established.

Bursting in and yelling "Eureka!" was not my best course of action.

What was worse, if a large team were to track down the places I'd seen, would this Lanie woman sense it, like she had with the Great Swamp? If she did, she might get Lindwall away before we could nail down the final location.

Great Piece Meadows was only about ten miles away. If I scouted out the area, maybe I could find that farmhouse.

I would need to block any psychic connection I might have with Lanie to make sure she couldn't read me.

Fortunately, I had just the thing. I got some water from the canteen and took a Percocet 2.5 mg tablet that I had with me.

For nighttime, I had a stronger prescription to help me sleep, but kept it at home. Right now, I just wanted something to help with my aching leg and to shut down my extra senses.

I threw away the empty cup and rolled out to the parking lot to get into my van and go scouting. I had a rough locale, and there really were not that many roads around the Preserve. If I had enough daylight left, I might track down the house.

I considered texting McGee, and even Jyanette, but dismissed both. McGee would insist that someone go with me. That would eliminate the stealthy approach. I also didn't text Jyanette as she always hated me going off on my own. Letting her know my plan would only ensure that I made her angry. She might not be my girlfriend, but I still didn't want to tick her off.

Once I got myself and the chair into my van and waited for it to warm up, I sent a quick text to Kate:

Checking out a lead near the Great Piece Meadows
I'll let you know if I find something

I figured that Kate would at least give me a chance to explore, and if she didn't hear from me, she could call in the cavalry.

I got an immediate reply:

I hope you know what you're doing

I wanted to text back, "Do I ever?" but, I didn't think that would be helpful.

I set the map app to give me directions and I started to drive. I traveled up Bloomdale Avenue, linking onto Route 23. Businesses were on my right and left; jewelry stores, pharmacies, even garden centers. I then took a left into a neighborhood of some of the biggest and most expensive houses one could imagine.

February is a difficult time of year. The excitement of Christmas and New Year is long past. It gets dark by five, the trees are barren, and everyone grumbles about winter weather. This year we hadn't had a lot of snow, so the dying grass and hibernating trees and bushes gave everything a sad look.

Even in the area I was driving through, with houses on hills with stone walls or hiding behind high wooden fences, everything had a heaviness, as if wanting winter to be over.

Of course, Lindwall had planned well. It was an easy way to spread a killer virus if everyone had to get indoors and into a warm place.

A few more turns and I was driving with the Passaic River on my right, past housing developments with names like, "Fairfield Estates" and "High Ridge" suggesting nice homes far from the annoying rabble. I passed an old stone house with a small blue sign that reported it was an historic site. From the neglect, it appeared that no one had gone near it in decades.

The road moved away from the river and houses began to appear on my right. These were on small lots and not as fancy as the developments, but still not inexpensive.

As I crossed over Route 46, shopping centers appeared and the traffic increased. Following my route, it soon returned to residential and a simple two-lane road. I now had the river on my left, having crossed over it along the way.

I saw a white picket fence to my right, and a large plastic orange dragon stood in a yard marked with a sign:

O'Reilly's

Motor Homes and Sales

I pulled into the road, which was its own little circular cul-de-sac, and drove slowly around the park. I moved down the cracked asphalt roads, over faded yellow speed bumps spaced every few hundred feet.

Most of the houses were converted mobile homes, now placed on permanent foundations. Each house had a tiny parcel of land, and the many structures were practically on top of one another. Even so, the homes had different adornments, and those varied as I drove about.

It was startling just how different they all were. Some had fences, trellises, and even picture windows. Others had decks attached to the back of the residence. Many had the metal paneling of the original vehicle replaced with vinyl siding, while a few were simply the original trailer boosted up on cinderblocks.

Cars were parked on both sides of the choked roadway, as only a few houses possessed a detached garage. The cars were not new, and in fact the tiny lots and closeness of each site gave the entire place a cluttered, run-down look.

As I circled back to the front, there were several untethered RVs together in one section, where there were multiple connections for water, electricity, and sewage. These vehicles were still on wheels and able to be driven away. I surmised they had taken up residence in the park for a limited time.

I had the sinking realization that if I saw Lindwall's RV, I wouldn't recognize it. I had seen it from the inside, and only glimpsed it briefly from the outside when I touched the electrical connection at the Great Swamp. That experience had been so quick I doubted I could give an accurate description.

Add to that, with even the low dose of the opiate, my abilities would not work. I would have to go into the RVs to identify the right one, which, if Lindwall was within, could get me killed.

The FBI said they were checking out RV encampments in the area, but would they only go to camping grounds, or would they think to look in places like this?

The park office was in the front of the community near the entrance, with a convenient parking space, so I pulled in. It was right behind the large dragon, and even though it was constructed of heavy plastic, weather-worn, with green moss growing on one side, it was still in pretty good shape.

I couldn't imagine why it was here.

I soon had my wheelchair on the ground, and pulled around to go through a gate leading to the office. Like most of the homes, this was a double-wide trailer, so there were steps to get in.

I was in less pain since I'd had the Percocet, so I used my cane to push myself upright. Fortunately I was experienced going up the stairs from when my right leg was frozen. My left leg went first and then I pulled my right up, supporting it with the cane the entire time. This worked just as well as it did when it was inflexible.

I knocked on the office door, and a woman's voice responded. "Come in."

The office was pretty casual, more like walking into the woman's living room than a place of business. The carpeting was worn and I could see a sofa and large screen TV mounted to one wall.

Near the door was a desk with two chairs. On the wall behind the desk was a map of the site. The map listed each of the lots for every home by number, printed with a marker.

A middle-aged woman rose from the sofa as a game show blared. She was matronly, and wore a formless flowered dress, but she looked neat. Her hair was curly and a shade of brown that could not be her natural color. She hit a button on the remote in her hand, and the screen went dark.

"Sorry, I thought you were one of the tenants. We're kinda informal here."

She spoke with a thick New Jersey accent.

"I'm sorry to bother you," I told her, and pulled out my MPD identification card. "I was just wondering if you had any recent renters who needed an RV hookup."

"You wid the cops?" she asked, looking at my ID card with suspicion.

I thought fast. "Someone has been ripping off mobile home parks, and I wanted to be sure they weren't taking advantage of you."

She glanced at my card again. "You're a helluva long way from Mountainview."

"The investigation has moved to outside our jurisdiction."

"Okay," she said. "Can I offer you a drink, or a cawfee?"

"No thanks. Would it be all right if I sit?"

"Oh yeah, you're walkin' wid that cane. Go ahead, sit, sit! Like I told ya, we're informal here."

I sat down and breathed a sigh of relief. That short walk into the office had started my leg aching again.

She sat with a mug in her hand and sipped on the coffee as I waited.

"Ya get injured in the line of duty or somethin'?"

I smiled. "No, I had knee replacement surgery about a week or so ago."

"Jeez, you shouldn't be walking around on that. Ain't they got someone in better shape than you?"

"I'm an investigator. It's my job to do the 'legwork' for the police."

"Legwork, I get it."

I pulled out my phone in case I needed to make a quick note. "So, any new tenants or recent RV arrivals?"

"Tenants are always coming and going in this place. Y'know a mobile home park ain't for everyone. But our location is pretty convenient to New Yawk City and all."

"Have all the RVs in the lot been here a while?"

"Yeah, the Logans have the big black one. They've been here about six weeks. We had the Tylers here for a while, but they left last week."

"Any new tenants?"

"Every month we get new ones, every month somebody leaves. I'm tellin' ya, running this place is a lot of work. Drives my husband nuts, having to fix shit all day long."

I slipped my phone back into my pocket. Obviously, there was no information for me here.

I pushed myself up with my cane. "Thank you, Mrs. O'Reilly."

"Oh! I ain't an O'Reilly. Do I look Irish to you? That was the last owner. I'm Meg Clayton."

"I appreciate your time," I said as I pulled my wallet out. "Let me leave you my card, in case you see anything suspicious." Since I don't have any MPD cards, and only ones for teaching at GSU, it was emblazoned with my name and my occupation.

"Parapsychologist?" Mrs. Clayton exclaimed with a frown. "Are you one of them ghost-hunters?"

I hate being compared to the frauds people see on television, but I forced a smile before I answered.

"I help the police as an investigator, in whatever way I can."

"Well, you ought to meet Lanie."

I froze. "Lanie?"

"Yeah, Lanie Dane. Weird name, huh? She, like, believes in all that stuff. She did a reading on me, and I tell ya, it was spooky. The things she knew about me was just incredible. She made a believer outta me, I'll tell ya that."

"Is she a homeowner?"

"Nah, just a renter, but she gave notice. She's leaving in a couple of weeks."

I moved to the wall map of the site. "Can you tell me which unit she lives in?"

"Number 204. That's on Second Street, right off of Ambassador Drive." She pointed to a rectangle with 204 scrawled in black marker.

"Does she drive a bright green car?" I asked, my throat tight.

She looked over at me. "Yeah, she does. Hey, you don' think she's involved in anything bad do you?"

I shook my head. "No, nothing like that. I think she's the ex-wife of a friend of mine."

"I tell ya, she's always been real nice to me."

"I'm sure it's not a problem. I might come back later, maybe with an officer, would that be all right?"

She shrugged. "The more the merrier, I say."

"You've been very kind," I said and headed for the door.

I was glad to get outside, down the stairs, and carefully return to my wheelchair. It had never felt so comfortable before.

I slowly trundled my way back to the van, wondering if it could be the same Lanie, or just a remarkable bit of serendipity. Carl Jung suggested that there were no coincidences. One of his quotes from my studies flashed through my mind: "Synchronicity is the coming together of inner and outer events in a way that cannot be explained by cause and effect and that is meaningful to the observer."

I got myself into the van's lift and into the driver's position.

I headed toward the main road and turned off onto Second Street. It was a little difficult to figure out which lot was the one Mrs. Clayton had pointed out, as the houses bore no numbers. Fortunately, I had quickly counted the number of houses when I looked at the map, and now I saw what looked like the correct address on my left.

There was no sign of the bright green car. If it was her, Lanie was probably with Lindwall.

I decided to return later, to see if the car showed up. In the meantime, while I still had daylight, I wanted to keep looking for the farmhouse from Johnson's memory, with the path behind it into the woods.

I drove out of the mobile home park and headed north again towards Great Piece Meadows.

As I crossed over the Passaic River a second time, it was as if I'd hit a switch. The route transformed into a simple road with woods on both sides, which meant I was getting close to the Preserve. I drove through a canopy of branches overhead, with a deep layer of brown leaves on both sides of the road. I passed the open green fields of the golf course, and couldn't help but wonder how they kept them so green in February.

The trees on the right side of the road ceased, and I could see the Golf Club clubhouse, and farther down the street, the huge building that was the church I had glimpsed in Johnson's mind.

It was an enormous structure, with at least two stories on the large main building as well as a newer addition. It was all white, with pillars supporting the side that faced the road, and it looked imposing rising up high from the large parking lot.

I could see why it stuck out in Johnson's mind.

I continued up the road, following acres of golf course all laid out on my right. On the left was nothing but woods, the Eastern side of the Preserve.

I peeked at a house through the trees on the left, but as I got close it wasn't right. It was too big and too modern.

Soon suburbia appeared on my left side, with houses, cars, and well-kept lots of land. The golf course gave way to nothing but woods. I did pass a few large modern houses, and their lots bordered the Preserve, but there were not many.

I was coming up on a house that wasn't built further back like the more modern ones, but practically right on the street. It was a large brown house covered in faded wood shingles. I slowed down as best I could. There was a car parked in front of a large wooden fence, keeping prying eyes from looking at the rear of the house, or any of the property behind the structure.

A plain white foreign hatchback was parked directly in front of the fence and blocked a wide gate made from the same tall fencing.

I continued past it until I was able to pull into a side street and turn around to view the house from the other angle. As I passed, I caught a glimpse of the back yard, and saw a clearing through the trees that led into the forest that backed the property.

I pulled onto a side road that featured parking for a large condo complex on the other side of the street. I positioned my van in one of the numerous parking spaces and considered what to do.

The idea that I could just roll over there in my wheelchair to look around was ridiculous. The house looked similar to what I had glimpsed in Johnson's head, but I couldn't be sure. With the Percocet in my system, I couldn't reach out with my mind to get a reading.

I made a note of the address on my phone and decided I should explore another way into the Preserve, just in case. I checked the map app and found an area next to the Preserve on a side street that was a little more out of the way. I decided to check it out now while it was still daylight.

Driving back, I was frustrated at how helpless I felt. The morning raid on the utility shed at the Great Swamp hadn't caught them, but even Agent Calvin had to admit an RV had been there in the morning. The APB on Lindwall's men had netted us Derrick Johnson, but he'd been little help.

How close were they to being able to release the virus? The question nagged at me.

The map led me off the main road and into an industrial park of tall concrete buildings, which led me to believe I had made a mistake. The road grew narrower, and houses appeared on both sides of the street. I pulled down a side road that backed right onto the Preserve and continued my search for the old brown house.

The residences on this side lane were all new houses, built within the last twenty years or so. Far too modern for the vision I glimpsed. One house had a lawn decorated with every mode of transportation that existed. There was a boat, several trailers, a pickup truck, and the cab of an eighteen-wheeler, all crammed onto the littered lawn.

Further down the road, a large chain link gate blocked my path. It must be an access road only used by the maintenance crew of the Preserve.

I pulled up to the fence and peered beyond it, but there were no houses that I could see.

I headed back the way I came and at the juncture, I noticed that the lane I had taken had a small extension past the main road. This extension was barely one lane, in bad repair, and there didn't appear to be any houses down it. I ignored it and took the route back toward the industrial park I had passed through.

I pulled into one of the huge buildings with an immense parking lot and sat there for a moment. I thought about the brown house I had passed, and how much it resembled the one I had glimpsed in Johnson's mind. There certainly was no way I could check the property in a wheelchair, and the clock was ticking…with dire consequences.

I pulled my phone from my pocket and texted McGee:

I might have a location where Lindwall parked his RV

I sent him the address I had noted and described the home.

McGee quickly sent a reply:

Is this credible?

I answered in the affirmative, and McGee let me know they would assemble a strike team to descend upon the location. I responded that I would be nearby.

I drove back to the condominium parking lot across the street from the building I had visited earlier. There, I could watch the house and keep an eye out for anyone leaving before the raid.

I hoped like hell I was right.

10. FALSE INFIRMITY

From my vantage point just down the road from the brown shingled house, I waited, wishing I had a pair of binoculars to get a better view. Daylight had faded into twilight, and now darkness fell. It was only 5:30, but winter days are always short.

The effect of the Percocet was fading. This meant my leg hurt a lot more, but my mental abilities were slowly returning and I might be able to do a reading on the house soon.

A light glimmered within the house as darkness descended, but I was unable to tell if someone turned it on, or if it had been on all along.

I sighed and looked at my watch. I didn't know what I had expected. McGee and ten SWAT team vans surrounding the neighborhood? This location was ten miles from MPD, and they had to get organized and maybe even come up with a plan. I was just wandering around in a van, trying to track down the unusual images I'd seen.

I began to think about the implications of capturing Lindwall. It would mean that their terrorist plot would be ended. It also meant that Jyanette would head back to Washington, continue dating Agent Calvin, and I would never see her again.

That concept burned like an icicle in my heart. How many times could I lose the same person, and have it hurt so much? I wanted to move on with my life, but the idea of doing it without her seemed dark and lonely.

What would I do? Go back to the occasional tryst with Kate? She was a contradiction to me as well. On one hand, she'd been acting possessive, and on the other, she was the one who'd kept the relationship casual.

I had to admit, I was tired of casual. I was thirty-one years old, and a man who enjoyed commitment. I wanted to build a future, not just enjoy recreational sex when the mood struck me.

Maybe that makes me unusual.

If not for the accident, Cathy and I would be celebrating our ninth anniversary. That's what I had wanted, but the accident took her life.

Then I met Jyanette and my world changed. I had loved Cathy, but Jyanette struck me like a force of nature. When she told me of the pregnancy, I asked her, *begged* her, to marry me. She'd even said yes once, and I bought an engagement ring. Then tragedy struck, and she was gone.

I still had the ring in one of the drawers of the desk in my sitting room, not having the heart to return it.

I was tired of loss, tired of not having a stable, dependable relationship. Even if Kate was interested in a steady romance, I didn't think that we would work well as a couple. As colleagues and friends, yes; but engaged, or married? I just didn't see it working out.

As I mused about the course of my life, a police car appeared, followed by one of the large SWAT vans I'd seen at MPD. The van went past the house then stopped. In a few short moves it was blocking the road.

I guessed that the police car went ahead to shut off the road near a turn off to direct traffic. There was probably another police car blocking this part of the road at the last intersection.

Efficient.

I pulled my winter coat around me, opened the door, and was lowered to street level. It had grown colder since the sun had set, and I wrestled the wheelchair out the side door. I wheeled my way a little closer, so I could be seen by McGee if he needed me.

The black-clad team members flowed out of the back of the van, the reflective lettering of "HOMELAND SECURITY" or "FBI" on their protective vests.

They moved towards the farmhouse and split into three groups. One group headed for the tall wooden fence to cover the back of the house. A second team went past the front of the house, to cover the addition and anyone escaping out the side. The final team moved to the front door. Two men were carrying a long black metal cylinder, which I decided could only be a battering ram.

Even from my position down the road, I heard the commander's yell of "HOMELAND SECURITY."

Without waiting for a reply, the two men swung the ram, and the door all but collapsed under the blow. A stun grenade was thrown in the open space, and there was a loud explosion and several screams from within.

With automatic weapons at the ready, the first team surged through the front door, as a loud explosion came from the back of the house, which I assumed was the second team setting off a stun grenade as well.

As the house was stormed, I saw two cars pull up and stop. One was McGee's unmarked, which I recognized, and the other was a black SUV. Gabe Petrie and Agent Marsh stepped out. McGee got out of his car, and I started to wheel down the street towards him.

The three men all wore heavy coats, and McGee broke from the group to move to me.

"I was getting concerned," I told him as we drew closer.

"We had to study the topography, see the best way to move in," McGee confessed. He moved behind me and began to push my chair. "Marsh insisted we attempt a satellite photo, and that took time."

"Did you see the RV?" I asked.

"The area behind this house has dense tree cover. We couldn't see if there was anything back there or not from all of the branches."

One of the helmeted men stepped out of the house and yelled. "Secure!"

Marsh and Petrie headed for the door, as McGee pushed me in that direction.

"You stay out here and I'll go in," McGee told me, as he abandoned my wheelchair at the front door. This probably made sense as I would only be in the way.

I heard voices, and a woman screaming angrily at the unwanted invaders. Then I heard another sound: children crying. I froze.

Would Lindwall have hidden himself in a place with kids nearby? Was he that much of a monster or did I pick the wrong place?

I heard the woman scream at the men, and the men talking and shouting at her, but it was impossible for me to make out what they were saying. I heard someone demand, "Where is Lindwall?" but I didn't hear a response.

The Percocet had worn off, and I closed my eyes, reached out, and touched the old farmhouse. A flood of images came into my mind: children growing up; a starter home for a new couple; people who had taken care of the house and people who didn't care about it at all.

It all shifted to a divorced woman, whose father had left her the place, doing her best to raise three kids on little money.

I didn't sense or see any evildoers, or white supremacists, or criminals.

Just a woman doing the best she could do.

I opened my eyes with a sick feeling in the pit of my stomach.

Lindwall had never been here.

I'd been wrong.

It was several hours before the FBI, Homeland Security, and MPD had everything straightened out. I tried to get to McGee, but he was too busy dealing with Petrie, Marsh, and the commander of the SWAT team to speak to me.

They moved the step van from the roadway into the spacious parking lot at the location, and removed the police cars that had blocked the road. This allowed traffic to go through again.

They also had men coming back out of the woods. The only vehicle they had found was the remains of what was reported to be a 1938 Studebaker. There were no fresh tire tracks into the woods from the rear of the house, and the wet ground would have left impressions.

From what I heard later, Marsh, Petrie, and McGee all apologized to the woman, and a carpenter and a locksmith were contacted to come right out and replace the woman's front and rear doors that had been destroyed with the battering rams.

The three men also discussed the situation outside, at, I noticed, a purposeful distance from me.

Finally Marsh and Petrie headed for the car they'd arrived in, which was parked on the side of the street. The last thing Marsh did as he crossed the road was to point at me. "That man is no longer on the team," he stated clearly.

I can't say I was surprised by this outcome.

McGee hung his head and moved towards me.

"I guess I blew this one," I said.

"Big time, I'm afraid," McGee sighed. "You need a ride to your van?"

"No, just push me into traffic and let nature take its course," I muttered. "I'm sorry, Bill."

Bill got behind me and began to push my chair. I was shivering by now, having been outside in the cold for the last few hours.

"What happened? How did you miss, and miss so big?"

"I read Johnson's mind, saw images from this area: a church, a golf course, even a mobile home park. There was also an image of a house that looked a lot like this one. It seems that I was wrong."

"This was a hell of a snafu, and there'll be hell to pay tomorrow. I'll be lucky if they keep *me* on the team."

I frowned. "Could you lose your job? Or your rank?"

"I doubt it. I've closed a lot of cases, and the detective squad is running better than it ever has. It appears that myself as lieutenant and Tice as Sergeant of Detectives is a good combination. Who'd have seen that coming?"

Another worrisome thought crossed my mind. "What about Jyanette? Are they going to hold my screw-up against her?"

"I don't know, Len."

I muttered, "She came by to visit me."

"Oh?" McGee replied, obviously surprised. "Any chance she'll reconsider your relationship?"

"I doubt it. She's dating Agent Calvin."

"Really?"

"Yes, and he came by and told me he only let me be on this case because he wanted to see what I was like."

"That seems a little paranoid for a federal agent," McGee fretted. He pointed toward the nearby condominium complex. "Is that your van up in the lot?"

"Yes," I answered, and McGee pushed me in silence as we approached the van. "I think having me off the team is a good choice."

"So, you had a screw-up. We've all had them. You can't blame yourself, Len."

We reached the van, McGee released the back of my chair and I spun it to look up at him.

"Bill, you know better than anyone how many times I've missed—"

"I also know how many times you've found things that helped. Look, I have to get back to MPD and try to make sure that we keep pushing to find this guy and his team."

"Sorry I let you down."

"Maybe you need to take a few days off. My guess is the painkillers are affecting what you do. We'll just have to do this with the assets we have."

"Do you think it will be enough?"

He shrugged. "It'll have to be. Keep in touch, Len."

I nodded as Bill turned around and headed back to his unmarked police car. I got the doors open and the lift down and was only too happy to start the van. I was still shivering and needed to get some heat going before I tried to drive on this cold night.

I pulled onto the road and realized I had one more place I needed to go. One last clue that might get me information that would make a difference.

Heading south, I took the fork to go over the river and in a few short minutes, I pulled back into O'Reilly's Motor Home Park.

By then the heat in my van was on, and I had it cranked up to get my fingers and toes all toasty. A little longer outside the old farmhouse and I could have developed hypothermia.

I shut off my headlights as I drove down Second Street.

Once I was at the far end of the street, I threw the van into park so I could observe the house I had been told was rented by Lanie.

The one-story mobile home was dark, not a light on in the place. I glanced at the clock on the dashboard and noted that it was almost ten o'clock.

Had coming here been a fool's errand, or was I on to something? She would probably stay with Lindwall, wherever he was holed up. By now, in all likelihood, they had to know that Johnson was captured by the police, and that they would have to make their move soon.

Perhaps even tonight...

Just as that thought struck me, turning my blood to ice, I saw a small car come around the corner with its headlights on. I slid down so I wouldn't be revealed in the flash of light, and cursed as my leg cramped up. I lay down and rubbed the leg to ease the cramp and pains I had up and down the limb.

I raised my head to see the small car had parked right under a streetlight.

It was a green car.

The driver got out, stood up, and I saw it was Lanie from my vision.

She appeared to stumble a bit, and I thought perhaps she had been drinking. Or she may be putting on an act, just in case anyone was watching.

I lowered my head out of sight and thought of a white wall, nothing but white. If this lady was at my level of psychic ability or higher, she might be able to sense my presence. Her stumbling could have been a ploy, so she could scan the area and sense if she were being watched.

I thought of nothing but white, putting all other thoughts out of my mind.

I waited…

After several minutes, I raised my head. The street was empty. I looked over at the bungalow, to see several lights burned behind the windows.

Now what to do?

I looked at the mobile home as ideas ran through my mind. Call McGee or maybe Kate?

No.

I scanned the numbers on my phone and pressed the button to place a call.

"Tice. Who's this?"

"It's Leonard Wise. I'm outside the place where your ex-wife is renting a mobile home."

My phone was silent. I wasn't sure if Tice would hang up, curse me, or even arrest me for all I knew.

"Hello?" I finally asked.

"Tell me where you are and how to get there."

11. QUALMS FLY ABOUT

It took Tice all of thirty minutes to arrive at the mobile home park.

At least I believed it was him, as I had never seen his car before. He did a slow circle and parked in front of me.

"Geez, Wise," Tice hissed, his breath steaming as he lumbered up to my open van window. "You're out here in the open? You're about as subtle as a toothache. Which house is it?"

"The one with the blue around the roof."

He stared up at the houses. "How can you tell in this light?" He examined his choices a second time. "Third from the corner?"

"That's the one. Step back, I need to get out."

I shut off the van and opened my door, hitting the button for the lift, which sounded incredibly loud on the silent street. I reached the ground and stood, using my cane for support. As the lift retracted, I started to pull the wheelchair from the side door.

"Let me do it," Tice grumbled. He easily lifted it out, placed it on the ground, and unfolded it. I gratefully sat down.

"So just us, then?" Tice asked.

"Did you hear about the raid?"

"A few rumors. I heard you're not on the team anymore. What happened, your mojo dry up?"

"Something like that," I replied. "But I found out about her living here earlier in the day, and I figured this would be easier if *you* went in."

He looked down at me and shook his head. "I still don't think she has anything to do with this."

"I understand, but you can talk to her. Lately, I've been missing the mark."

A small grin appeared on his face. "How the mighty have fallen."

"Nice, Tice. Hit a man when he's down, why don't you?"

"I dunno, Doc. It kind of makes you a little more human."

"Yeah, when do *you* start?" I grumbled.

His grin faded. He didn't like it turned back on him. He looked up at the house. "You're sure it's her?"

"I saw her before she went in. And it was strange, she stumbled a bit."

"Stumbled?"

"Like she'd been drinking. I don't know, it could have been a way to sneak a look down the street."

"She *is* a smart lady."

"If you knock on the door and talk to her, it's the best way to find out if she's involved."

"Or if it even *is* her," Tice muttered. His hand automatically went to the shoulder holster under his suit jacket to touch his weapon for reassurance.

He began to walk toward the home, and I wheeled up behind him.

He turned to face me. "Where are you going, Doc?"

"Look, Tice, I think this lady can do what I do and maybe more," I explained. "I'll be outside of the house and if I get any warnings, I'll yell to you."

His mouth twisted into a sneer. "Warnings? Oh, yeah, those 'buzz' things you told McGee about. That's all a lot of hooey."

"Hooey?" I repeated.

"It sounded better than bullshit."

"Tice, I'll stay outside, but I feel like I should be there. To be... I guess... your backup."

Tice turned away and shook his head in disbelief. "The day you're my backup is a dark day for me."

He started to walk again and I rolled my chair to keep up.

"Would you prefer that the FBI were here, smashing down your ex-wife's door? That's why I called you. I think you can help her."

"Like she ever listened to me," Tice grumbled, as we reached the sidewalk that led to the front of the home. It was a short pavement that ended at three stairs to reach the doorway. Tice went up the steps and knocked on the steel entry door.

I waited on the sidewalk, moving the chair so I couldn't be seen from the windows.

Tice knocked a second time and called out "Alaina? It's Joe."

He then knocked again.

"Joe?" a woman's voice called out. I recognized the sound from the vision I'd seen at the RV with Lindwall. "What are you doing here?"

"We need to talk," Tice said, not as loudly.

"The door's open, come in," was the reply.

Tice glanced at me and turned the knob. The door opened a crack as I tried to reach out with all my senses. It was quiet, but not silent. Air whispered through the building's heating system. The refrigerator compressor hummed as it switched on inside the kitchen.

Tice stood in the open door and said, "Okay, I'm coming in."

DANGER...

When I get a buzz, it is often just a little thing to get my attention, but when it screams in my head, I know there is a real problem.

"Tice!" I yelled. "Hit the deck."

Tice glanced in my direction, and then, without a moment of hesitation, he dove to the floor, just as an explosion shattered the still country air and reverberated in my ears. It wasn't the sound of a handgun, it had to be a shotgun at the very least and possibly a cannon.

I wheeled my chair towards the road yelling, "Stay down, Tice."

The second blast detonated right behind me and I lowered my head into my lap and covered it with my hands as debris, chunks of siding, wood, and glass rained down on me. I stopped and looked back to see a gaping hole in the wall of the home, right where I had been moments earlier.

Though my ears were still ringing, I heard Tice, but couldn't see him. "Lanie, put it down or I'll shoot. Don't make me shoot you, Lanie! Please!"

And then I caught her voice. "Joe? Is it really you, Joe? I thought you were Lindwall."

Through the hole in the wall I saw a double-barreled shotgun fall to the floor.

I carefully peered in to see Lanie go down on one knee. The rifle was close to the hole, so I reached in and pulled it out and into my lap. At the time, I figured it was the best choice. Get the gun away from the crazy person who wants to shoot you.

Tice went to Lanie, and helped her to her feet.

"Joe," she gasped. "I thought you were Lindwall, coming to kill me."

"Lanie, what's this all about?" Tice said, holding her close.

"Deep cover," Lanie said and seemed to have trouble drawing breath. "I infiltrated the Faction."

"Lanie, I thought you stopped working for the Feds after we divorced."

"No, Joe," she said. "I had to go deep cover to get involved... had to find out how they planned to use the virus."

"What happened?"

"They found out I was FBI." All at once, she pushed Tice away. "Get back."

"Why?" Tice said, his arms open to her.

"They exposed me to the virus, sprayed some of it right on me," she replied, her hand went to her face.

"But why come here? Why didn't they get you to a safe house?"

"I called my superior. He told me to come here, so I could be evacuated safely. But I felt I was followed... watched. I thought Lindwall was after me, planning to kill me." She sat on the arm of a nearby sofa. "Joe, I don't feel so good, I'm so hot."

DANGER...

And in my mind I saw it. There was something inside of Lanie and it was killing her.

"Tice, call an ambulance," I yelled.

"What?" Tice yelled back, annoyed.

"For God's sake, she's *infected.*"

"Hands in the air, punk," a voice growled.

I froze and slowly lifted my hands.

"Throw the gun on the ground," the voice threatened.

Only moving my head, I glanced over to see a man in some kind of uniform with a heavy coat, white shirt, dark pants, and a hat like a police officer on his head. He was short and chunky, and had a mustache, but the thing I noticed the most was the large handgun he held with the barrel pointed at my head.

"I—it's not my gun," I said, at a loss for breath. "I took it away from the woman who fired it."

"Then drop it on the ground," he ordered.

"I will, I will," I said, and slowly lowered one hand to push the shotgun away.

I had a moment of blind panic where I thought the gun might discharge when it hit the ground and the security guy was going to shoot me. I would never get to try out my new knee, I would never see Jyanette, or even McGee, again.

The gun fell to the ground in silence, both barrels having been emptied.

I lowered my hands, again very slowly, to the wheels of my chair and rolled back, away from the weapon.

Sirens wailed in the distance.

The short man lowered the pistol and slipped it into a holster on his belt. Then he bent to grab the shotgun.

Danger…

"Don't touch that," I said and he stood up.

"Why not?"

"It might be infected. You should only pick it up with gloves and seal it or something."

He looked down at the shotgun and then at me. "What the Hell is going on in there?"

"I have identification," I said, my hands back up in the air. "I'm with the Mountainview Police Department."

"Let's see!"

He watched me suspiciously, as I slowly pulled out my billfold with the MPD card and opened it. He reached for it and I pulled it back. "Wait, I might be infected, too."

He stepped back. "What are you talking about?"

"The man inside is a police detective from Mountainview. I was assisting him."

"I'll have to see his ID as well," the man said.

"No sir," I snapped.

He frowned. "What?"

"The woman inside has been exposed to a highly infectious virus. I need you to keep everyone back while I make a phone call."

"Buddy, I didn't read the fine print on your ID, but it said you're a civilian consultant. How do you get off giving me orders?"

I stared at the man and reached into his mind, only a little, as I snarled, "If you don't keep people back, they will all die."

He blinked a few times and looked around to see that people had come out of the other houses on the block. He yelled over to them, "Get inside folks, we got this under control."

I turned away and pulled my phone from my pocket. I quickly looked up the number for McGee and hit it.

"Not a good time," he answered the phone tersely.

"McGee, we've got Lanie. The woman I saw in the vision."

"Wait," he said. "Who is we?"

"Me and Tice. He's with her."

"Great, bring her in for questioning."

"We can't, Bill. She's infected."

"What? How?"

"Don't tell anyone, but I think she's undercover FBI. They found out, and they exposed her to the virus. I think they used her to test it."

There was silence on the phone for a moment, and then Bill asked, "Did you get exposed?"

I looked at the hole in the wall, and thought about grabbing the gun she'd just touched, and really wished I had some hand sanitizer about now.

"I'm not sure if I was, but Tice definitely has been exposed."

"I'll get the hazmat team moving. Where are you?"

I told him and hung up the phone. In the distance I saw the flashing lights and heard the wail of approaching sirens.

12. DISTRACTING DISEASE

The security man, whose name I never did learn, talked to the police and probably told them I was some kind of nut. The police unit that arrived was the Fairfield Township Police and I was able to persuade them to contact the Mountainview Police and speak to the captain. I also acted to relay messages from Tice who was still inside the house, who told me that Lanie had fallen unconscious.

It took about forty minutes, but one of the big mobile laboratories arrived, escorted by a SWAT team step van and two MPD cars with lights flashing. The lab was so big I wondered how the hell they had made the turns to even get it into the mobile home park.

Several cars arrived and both Agents Marsh and Calvin were there, as well as Gabe Petrie.

There was no sign of McGee.

I was getting pretty cold again, but I stayed put, as men and women in what looked like space suits came out of the lab. The suits were bright yellow, and covered them from head to foot. A large, clear plastic faceplate allowed me to see the person inside, and each one was wearing a respirator. There was a tank on each person's back, providing them with an individual air supply.

The yellow-clad people began to set up a series of small tents in the street next to the bungalow. It was truly amazing. First they laid a tarpaulin on the ground, then a framework for each one was quickly unfolded and raised into the air with supports. Finally, they unfolded flooring and hung cloth to form flaps for the openings.

It was as if an army had taken over the area. Men climbed up telephone poles and ran electric lines to the lab. Long thick cords connected the lab to the small tents.

Another man hooked up a water supply from a fire hydrant, and a hose snaked out of the lab and was attached to connectors in the tents.

What alarmed me most were the black helmeted soldiers going house to house to evacuate the residents as quickly as possible. They weren't letting people drive off on their own, but herding them all, men, women, and children into another step van. They were being shipped out to facilities being set up to temporarily house and test them, to see if they had been exposed.

The entire thing was Orwellian in the extreme, and beyond anything I could imagine. I sat there shivering. This is what the entire town of Mountainview could be transformed into if Lindwall succeeded in releasing the virus.

That thought was more chilling than the cold weather.

Two men in the yellow outfits, which I recalled were called an "encapsulation suit," approached me. One man sprayed the shotgun that lay on the ground near me. He then picked it up and headed for the first tent.

The second man moved right to me, went down on one knee, and spoke to me, his voice coming through a tinny speaker on a side bag he carried.

"Are you Doctor Wise?"

I nodded.

"How are you feeling?"

I attempted a smile, but it was half-hearted at best. "I'm c-cold."

"I am going to wheel you into the decontamination tent. Will you be able to stand without your chair or your cane, if I help you?"

"Y-yes."

"Good."

He got behind me and pushed my chair into the first tent the team had set up. The tent was supported by a metal frame, and a large box was blowing out hot air, heating the small enclosure.

The man helped me to my feet and I leaned on the supporting framework as my chair was grabbed by a woman in another encapsulation suit. She pulled the chair to the far side of the structure and began to spray it down with a nozzle. A bottle was connected to the sprayers so some kind of disinfectant was being used on my chair and cobra-head cane.

"Doctor Wise, pull out your wallet, phone, keys, and anything else, and put it in that box there."

He gestured to a small army-green box. He then pointed at a large green open box on the floor. "In that container, put your clothes."

"My clothes?" I repeated.

"Yes, all of your clothes: shoes, socks, underwear, everything."

I went through my pockets and placed my ID, phone, and keys in the small box, just as Tice came into the tent followed by Lanie on a stretcher.

The man who had helped me pulled out a second small box for Tice's things, as well as added instructions for Tice to place his firearm on a standing metal rack that was designed to hold guns.

I had pulled my winter coat off and was removing my sports coat as he began to undress.

"You okay, Tice?" I asked.

He looked at me very seriously. "Yeah, Doc. Thanks to you. Lanie didn't mean to shoot at either of us. She thought Lindwall had come to finish her off. I think she was delirious."

He looked over at Lanie, and I could see the concern written on his face, as well as affection.

The two men who had carried her in on the stretcher were now focused on Lanie, which was a very different circumstance. They were using scissors and *cutting* her out of her clothes.

They worked very quickly, and I turned away, embarrassed by the fact that in moments she would be stark naked.

Fortunately my shoes were slip-ons so I got out of them, but getting my sock off and remaining upright was difficult. Finally Tice looked over, and even though he was only in his underwear, he dropped to one knee and hissed. "Hold still, I'll get it."

"Thanks, Tice," I said as he pulled my socks off.

"Can you manage your pants?" he muttered.

"I hope so. My leg isn't very strong, yet."

He sighed. "You lean on me, okay?"

I nodded. I leaned on his shoulder as I pulled out my left leg from the trousers. Then out came my right leg.

"For the love of God," Tice gasped, his eyes focused on the twisted flesh of my leg.

"I know, it's not pretty," I said.

"Did this new knee help or make it worse?"

"It will be better, but it is kind of ugly right now."

I got my feet under me, and Tice and I continued to remove clothing.

Lanie was now completely undressed on the stretcher and the team was spraying her and sponging her body down. In a delirium, she attempted to fight them off, the spray of water reviving her a bit.

By now, Tice and I were also naked, modesty apparently had no place here. The man with the sprayer hosed us down and the woman gave us a pair of sponges and told us to wipe it all over our bodies. It contained something that left a light foam everywhere it touched. Once we were done, we put the sponge into a plastic bag and the man with the sprayer showered us with a high pressure stream of water.

Our final course of action was to step into a foot washing box, and we went into the next tent still dripping.

They had moved Lanie to a gurney instead of a stretcher. She had a blanket wrapped tightly around her and a man in scrubs, gloves, and a surgical mask was examining her. A nurse, also in scrubs, gloves, mask, and gown handed Tice and me towels, and I dried myself as best I could.

"Okay, move her out," the doctor said, as two men in the same protective clothing came in and moved the gurney away. He yanked off his gloves, as the nurse held out a new pair which he pulled on and turned to us.

"Either of you feel sick?" he asked looking from me to Tice. At the same time, the nurse pointed a hands-free thermometer, first at Tice and then me.

"I'm right as rain," Tice replied, stone-faced. "She collapsed on me, though."

The doctor was looking at Tice but not touching him. "Look up please. Open your mouth."

"Doctor, this man's temperature is very low," the nurse said after pointing the thermometer at me.

The doctor turned from Tice and looked at the reading on the thermometer. "Christ, how long were you out there, man?"

"It's been a night," was all I could manage.

"Open your mouth, and look up."

I did as I was told.

"All right, get them both into isolation and tell them to treat this man for hypothermia." The nurse pointed at the flap that led to the third tent.

We passed two men in army fatigues with face masks and plexiglass shields. They both wore nitrile gloves and stood next to a large locker with many shelves. They quickly pulled out green underwear and fatigues and pointed to a bench.

Tice and I got dressed, and I was impressed that the clothing they'd selected fit my tall, lanky frame very well. They even had canvas shoes for my size 14 feet.

A man stepped into the tent, also in fatigues, a mask, and plexiglas shield, but I saw captain's bars on his collar. He was followed by Agents Marsh and Calvin who also wore protective clothing.

"Which one of you gets the wheelchair and the cane?" the captain said.

I raised my hand.

"We will hold them for you and have them taken to the hospital, where you both will be put in isolation."

"Isolation?" Tice repeated.

"Is that necessary?" I asked.

He went on as if I had said nothing. "All of your personal effects will be tested, sanitized, and returned to you there as well."

Marsh stepped forward. "Thank you, Captain, we'll take it from here."

The captain nodded and he and the two other men left the tent, leaving us alone with the FBI agents.

"As the captain said," Marsh explained, "you've both been exposed. You are being moved to an isolated ward at the Mountainside Medical Center."

"What's happening with Alaina?" Tice demanded.

"She told us that she's FBI!" I barked. "Someone blew her cover."

Marsh and Calvin exchanged a look.

"Right now, she's being treated," Marsh explained. "We are aware that she's undercover. The Bureau has been working with her for months as she infiltrated the Faction. I want you two men to tell no one of her status."

I kept going. "They exposed her to the virus."

"Yes," Marsh replied coldly. "If we have any luck, we can find a cure."

"What if you're not lucky?" Tice growled. "That's my ex-wife!"

Calvin pointed at Tice. "She had a job to do—"

"Either way," Marsh interrupted, "she's been exposed to the pathogen, and this might be our only opportunity to find something that can fight it."

Calvin stood up straighter and threw his shoulders back. "If her cover was exposed, that might mean we have to check people on the team who might have revealed her."

"What does that mean?" I demanded.

"It means we have to look at everyone who could have known," Calvin said. "And no one is above suspicion."

"What will you do with her house?" I asked.

Marsh turned to me. "These guys are putting a plastic tent over the whole thing, they'll seal it and sanitize it."

"The neighborhood is being evacuated and the residents tested," Calvin added.

Marsh leaned towards me. "Now, what I want to know is — how did you find her, Wise?"

"The old-fashioned way, by investigating. I spoke to the lady who runs this place. She mentioned someone named Lanie. I staked out her place, and she showed up."

Calvin glared at Tice. "And how did you happen to be here?"

"The Doc knew she was my ex, and he called me. Good thing, as Lanie had that shotgun, and would've taken out anybody that came to that door."

Marsh crossed his arms. "It's just funny how Doctor Wise happens to show up, and her cover is exposed."

"What are you suggesting?" I snapped.

"Nothing that isn't obvious," Marsh replied.

"Gentlemen," a voice came from behind me and we turned to see the doctor from tent two. "These men have to get into isolation right away. You can question them there to your heart's delight."

"Okay, come on," Marsh said.

Tice took a step forward, stopped, and then moved to my right side. "Lean on me, Doc. We can do this."

We walked out as a group to an awaiting ambulance, Tice helping me the entire way. My leg was beyond aching, and I was in agony at this point. I stumbled into the back of the vehicle, where an EMT in one of the sealed yellow hazmat suits helped me onto a stretcher, followed by Tice. Calvin closed the back doors, and the vehicle began to move.

The stretcher in this vehicle was unusual, as it had a plastic cover, held by a curved frame that ran the length of it. One side could be zipped closed with a temporary air supply from a tank on the frame. The EMT helped me lie down, but didn't close the large opening.

I was so weary and cold it was a miracle I could raise my head to see Tice as he lay down on the stretcher next to mine.

I looked over at him and said, "Thank you, Joseph."

"Don't mention it, Len," he replied. Then he raised his head and grinned at me. "I mean it, don't mention it… to anyone. You want to ruin my reputation as a hard-ass?"

I chuckled. "I wouldn't dream of it."

13. ISOLATION ILLNESS

I don't recall much once we arrived at the hospital. I had fallen asleep in the ambulance, was beyond exhausted, cold, and in a lot of pain.

Fortunately, since my knee surgery had been done at Mountainside, they had all of my medical records. Several people in yellow protective hazmat suits met our ambulance at an entrance I had never seen before. There was a pair of double doors that opened on a vestibule and a single elevator.

They insisted that Tice and I remain on the gurneys as the EMT who had ridden with us sealed the plastic coverings and started the compressed air flowing within.

The pair of us were lowered to the ground, as the team of yellow clad nurses and orderlies pulled us into the building. I assumed the elevator was specifically designed to bring in dangerous or infectious cases.

Once we were all in the large elevator, the door sealed with a hiss. As we went up, one of the team asked us questions about how we were feeling and how long our exposure had been. One of the nurses pointed a thermometer at our heads, and between questions, she said, "Doctor, this man has a low body temperature."

I had warmed up a bit in the ambulance, but still felt chilled.

"I was briefed that one patient was borderline hypothermic," the doctor replied. The door opened and we were whisked down a hallway.

At this point, Tice and I were separated and I was moved into an isolation area. It had an outer room with a pane of glass and a phone where someone could sit and talk to the patient without being in the room with them. The reception room had a small locker room where doctors and nurses could suit up before coming in to see the patient. On the floor in front of the patient's bedroom were red rectangles, which were the markers for the removal of PPE clothing and masks.

Once the gurney was in the room, one man remained as the others left. He opened the seal, shut off the air supply, and helped me to sit on the bed. He assisted me as I undressed, put the clothes back on the gurney, and helped me into a hospital gown and back under the covers.

He then sealed the gurney and rolled it away, as a nurse came in. She wasn't wearing a hazmat suit, but merely a disposable gown, mask, goggles, a head covering, shoe covers, and a double pair of gloves. As I lay in the bed she added several blankets and an IV was inserted into my arm.

The blankets had a cord, so I was sure they were electric ones designed to get my body temperature up. The nurse made sure the blanket was on, and took a moment to inject something into my IV. My guess was a strong dose of Demerol, because I was out of pain very quickly and soon dropped off to a dreamless sleep.

I awoke the next day in the hospital room. Sometime during the night, the electric blanket had been removed, and a plain hospital blanket had replaced it.

I raised myself into a sitting position. My cobra headed cane was leaning against the nearby table. On top of it were my wallet, keys, ID, and smart phone. I was sure all the items had been properly disinfected.

I grabbed my phone and opened the screen, glad it still had a charge of over fifty per cent. I called Bill.

McGee picked up on the first ring. "Len! Are you all right?"

"I'm in a hospital bed, but I'm awake. How's Tice?"

"I spoke to him earlier. He's not showing any symptoms at this time, but he has to remain in isolation."

"Do you know how long I'll be here?"

"They'll let you know."

"Have they been able to question Lanie?"

"She hasn't regained consciousness."

I was stunned. She'd been fine in my first vision. She said that Lindwall infected her when he found out she was with the FBI, but when? How long did it take for this virus to manifest? Had it only been a few hours by the time Tice and I got to her, or had it been longer?

"You did a great thing last night, Len. If she had died and someone found her, the infection could have spread throughout that trailer park."

"That's a scary thought. Maybe that was why Lindwall infected her instead of killing her."

"If you and Tice hadn't gone to her and alerted us, we'd be looking at full quarantine this morning."

I thought about that. Lanie had said her superior had told her to go to her trailer and that she would be evacuated from there. Why would an FBI agent tell her to go to such a populated location if she had been infected? He should have told her to isolate herself. It made no sense.

"So does Marsh still want me off the team?"

"He seems to like the idea that you're stuck at the hospital until they release you. Marsh and Calvin are talking about questioning you again."

"I guess being interrogated will be the high point of my day," I scoffed.

"Guess it will. I gotta go, we're reviewing what we know. If you do get a fix on where Lindwall is, call me."

I ended the call and stared at my phone. My leg was beginning to ache, but I still couldn't feel my extra senses, so I was still processing the drug out of my system. If the doctor put me on something and I was stuck here, there was little I could do to track down Lindwall or any one in his team.

"And how are we today?" a perky woman said as she came in the door. She wore a paper gown over her scrubs, double-gloving on her hands, a face mask, and a helmet with a plastic shield.

I felt like I wanted to give her a snippy reply, but I didn't want to annoy the staff, as it could only prolong my incarceration.

"We are fine. We are trying to find out if the doctors think I was exposed, as we would like to get out of here."

I couldn't keep the sarcasm out of my voice.

She pointed a hands-free thermometer at my head until it beeped. "Good, your temperature is nice and stable, and not going up."

"What was it when I was admitted last night?"

"About ninety-three degrees Fahrenheit."

"That's not good," I stated.

"Are you feeling hungry?"

"I could use some coffee and maybe something to eat."

"That's a good sign," she said in a delighted tone. "Now, would you like to get out of isolation?"

"Is there any chance?"

"I'll get you some breakfast, then I'll draw blood, do a nasal swab, and a few more tests to see if we can detect any virus. Are you okay with that?"

"I'm willing if it can get me out of here," I said.

"I'll get right on that. Are you up to a visitor?"

I all but jumped out of the bed. "Is it a tall African-American woman?"

"Why yes!" her eyes narrowed. "You must be psychic."

"You have no idea," I muttered. "Is there a mirror?"

"In the bathroom," she said and pointed at a closed door on the other side from the entrance. "Can you get there by yourself?"

I grabbed my cane and sat up. The IV was still in my arm, but the solution bag was on a wheeled stand.

"Yes, just give me a couple minutes."

"I'll get you that breakfast," she said and headed out the door.

I got up slowly, and with my cane in my right hand and the IV stand in the other I made my way into the bathroom, relieved myself, and used the water in the sink to get my tangle of hair into an acceptable form.

I looked haggard. I needed a shave, I had circles under my eyes, and I wasn't a pretty sight.

Doing what I could to clean up, I returned to the bed and was sitting up when I saw Jyanette through the window in the reception room.

She glanced at me through the glass, and I saw how tired she looked. Her eyes were puffy and I think she had been crying. Had it been over me?

She picked up the phone receiver on her side of the glass. A phone rang next to the bed and I picked it up and looked over at her.

"Hi," I said, finding that words escaped me.

I saw anger flash in her eyes. "And here you are, in a hospital *again*," she snapped.

"Jyanette, I didn't get beaten up or shot, though the woman *tried* to shoot me—"

"So I heard."

"I didn't go alone, I had Tice for backup! You really can't blame me for this."

She sighed. "No, I guess I can't. And it was a good save after that screwed-up raid, which I also heard about."

I was actually relieved. This was going better than I thought it would. "How are you?"

"Not getting much sleep, and here I am again, worried sick about you."

"I'm fine," I attempted.

"Your surgeon isn't thrilled that you're doing so much physical activity so soon after your knee replacement."

I frowned. "How do you know that?"

"Margery gave me the phone number for your doctor."

I was shocked. Mrs. Higgins sold me out! Whose side was she on?

"Jyanette, you've sat in on the meetings. You know better than anyone what will happen if this virus is released. People will die, and it could spread uncontrolled. I have to do what I can."

"There is a team of people, Len. We are all working to track Lindwall down."

"So, he's been captured?" I challenged her.

She glared knives at me. "No, and don't be so freakin' smug."

"Sorry, but this thing is weird. Can I tell you something and ask that you don't repeat it to Calvin? I was told not to say anything to anyone."

"About the case?"

"Yes. Lanie was working undercover for the FBI."

"What?"

"She was in bad shape last night and raving a bit, but that's what she was saying. Marsh backed it up."

"Len, that's impossible. If she were FBI, she would have a controller, someone in the Bureau running her. Once Lindwall's name came up, she should have been brought in and given us his whereabouts immediately."

"I don't know, but it is pretty odd," I said, and then I tried to tell her what I wanted to say. "I'm glad you wanted to see me."

She looked flustered by this. "I... couldn't stay away."

This was my opening. It was now or never. "Jyanette, why are we doing this, being apart? God, you're all I think about every day."

Her jaw tightened, and she turned away, unable to look at me. "I thought I had moved on... and yet here I am, worried about you."

"Look, I know you're seeing Agent Calvin—"

She waved her hand dismissively. "He told me the bone-headed stunt he tried, going to your house to confront you. I apologize for that. I think his testosterone was running a little too high and I told him so. He didn't take it well."

My heart gave a lurch and it was a wonder I didn't leap out of bed and attempt an Irish jig, IV and all.

"To be honest, I'm thrilled."

She glared at me. "This doesn't mean a thing about us, Len."

"I guess not," I replied, crestfallen.

She nibbled on her lower lip. "Look, you need to get well and get out of the hospital. I have to help solve this damn case."

"Before you go back to Washington, can we at least meet? Maybe talk?"

She considered it, and several emotions appeared on her face as she did. "Okay, one meeting, and then I'm on my way back to Virginia."

"You won't run off on me?"

"To be honest, I want to run off right now."

I grinned. "Okay, we'll meet and talk."

She glanced at her watch. "I have to get back... y'know?"

"I do."

She gave a tight little nod, put the phone back in the receiver, and waved at me as she left.

I lay on the bed, not quite knowing what I should feel. This was a chance, but it didn't do a damn thing to resolve the issues that made her leave in the first place.

I recalled the day she told me she was returning to Virginia with her parents. Her mother, Deka, walked up to me and hugged me. Then she whispered into my ear, "It is hard now, but you will be all right."

Deka was the daughter of a *Nganga,* an African healer, and had abilities that I was not quite sure about. Had she seen a future where I would be with Jyanette? Or was she speaking of another future, that had not yet unfolded for me?

As I pondered these thoughts, my nurse returned with a cart that had a plate of food on it, and a hypodermic, several vials for blood samples, and other implements of torture.

"Any trouble getting to the bathroom and back?" she asked, once again in her 'chipper' voice.

"None at all."

"Good!" She handed me an empty plastic screw-top container and pointed toward the bathroom. "Fill it."

Hours later, after I had been fed and caffeinated with terrible hospital coffee, I was able to persuade the nurse to remove the IV and to give me a non-opiate painkiller. She obliged with naproxen, which took the edge off my leg soreness, but wouldn't interfere with my psychic senses.

The blood, urine, nasal swab, skin sample, hair sample, and whatever else they took were being analyzed for traces of any virus. I was hoping the tests would come back negative. If they forced me to stay here, there would be little I could do to help in the real world.

Not that being stuck in a wheelchair allowed me to do much.

Fortunately, I made a call that I hoped would remove some of the limitations I was experiencing.

The hospital phone next to my bed rang and I looked at the visitor window to see my Teaching Assistant, Teddy Santos, through the glass.

I picked it up. "Teddy, you made it."

"Sure thing, Doc. How are you holding up?"

"As well as can be expected. Did you bring my laptop?"

"Yeah, it was in your van which I drove back to your house. Good thing you gave Mrs. H that spare key."

"How was driving it? I mean, with the brake and accelerator on the steering wheel."

"Scared the Hell out of me, but I took back roads and drove slow. I have to tell you, I was glad to get back into my own van."

Teddy had driven me in his fire-engine red van one time. It was a full-sized one, and about twenty years old.

"Is that clunker still running?"

"Like a champ, Doc. I brought the laptop bag which I gave to the nurse to be, like, sanitized or something, so she'll bring it to you." He gave a sly look around to make sure he was alone. "I also brought a bag of clothes Mrs. H put together in this backpack." He tapped the bag on his shoulder.

"Great! Can you slip that into the kneehole where you're sitting?" I asked.

He frowned. "Is that necessary? I mean, you're in isolation for a reason, right?"

"Trust me, Teddy. If I don't get a clean bill of health, I'll stay in here, I promise."

He took the bag and with one more glance, shoved it under the small shelf the phone rested upon and put it in deep so it was not easily seen.

"Thanks, Teddy, you're a life saver."

He lowered his head and put his hand over the mouthpiece. "What's this all about, Doc? Mrs. H doesn't know a thing."

"I can't talk about it."

"That's what Ben says."

"You still seeing Galland?" I asked. I knew that Teddy was bisexual and dated both men and women. He had been seeing Galland for the last few months.

"Not lately," Teddy said, disappointment in his voice. "I know that there's something going on and no one's talking about it."

"Me too, I'm afraid."

"Okay, well, I gotta get to class."

"Thanks for your help as always, Teddy."

He hung up, smiled and waved, then headed out, minus the backpack.

I only had Teddy for a few more months, as he would be graduating with a degree in Computer Sciences and a secondary degree in Parapsychology this coming spring. He had agreed to stay with me for the summer to train my new TA, who would be a freshman, Anna Sokolov. She and I had been meeting every few weeks over the last few months. It turns out the young woman had impressive psychic abilities, and I'd been giving her exercises to help her control them.

I had to admit, I would miss Teddy.

It took about a half-hour before my nurse reappeared and brought my laptop. Having studied medicine, I was well aware how every nurse in a hospital is required to take care of a large number of patients. The fact it only took a half-hour was what surprised me.

She brought in the laptop bag so I had the charger and the few accessories I carried with me.

"Thank you," I said as she laid the bag on my side table.

"The doctor will be coming by sometime this afternoon, and we should have the results from your tests," she reported.

"That's good news," I replied. "Any idea how they look?"

"I'll let the doctor tell you that."

I nodded. "Any word on Joseph Tice or Alaina Woods?"

"Really I'm not allowed to talk about other patients, Mister Wise."

"Actually, it's *Doctor* Wise."

Her eyebrows lifted. With the mask on, it was all I could see of her expressions. "Oh? That explains how you know so much."

I wasn't sure if she meant that sincerely or was being sarcastic, but she trotted out of the room before I could comment.

Inside the bag with my laptop was a small card which listed the hospital's wifi network and password.

Since it was my only chance to look at the outside world, I decided it would come in handy.

I booted up, and with only one or two mistakes was online. Somehow, I had been close to Lindwall's location the previous night, I felt it in my bones. With the use of modern technology, I might be able to retrace where I drove the previous day and perhaps I would be able to find the man himself, or his oversized RV.

I had grown up with computers my entire life, but now the things they could accomplish were remarkable. I decided to use an online map program with street view, which I felt might allow me to see the house I had been looking for, but had been mistaken the previous night.

Why not? Locked up in isolation, I had nothing but time.

There was only one road that actually went through the Great Piece Meadow Preserve, so I tried that. Going up and down Horseneck Road showed me nothing other than green scenery, as the photos on the site were shot during the summer. I was surprised that there were some houses in the Preserve, built many years ago before it had been taken over by the state.

I checked out a small dead end road that came off Horseneck, and there were houses, but none that looked like the one in my vision.

I tried a couple more roads on the Western side of the Preserve, but had very little luck. There were houses all around the area, yet none with those brown weather-worn shingles.

I was at it for about an hour, still with no luck. Finally, I went back to the places I had driven the previous day. My first visit was to the house the FBI had raided last night. It felt like it had been days ago instead of merely the previous evening.

The photos showed it in summertime, and the greenery around it made it look much nicer than the actual house I had seen. I retraced my steps to take me to that road beyond the corporate park, where it had been shut off as it entered the Great Piece Meadow.

Yesterday, on my smart phone screen, the fence was the last place listed on that particular road, although there was a roadway beyond that went into the Great Piece Meadow itself. When I was actually there, I recalled there didn't appear to be any houses on that closed access road.

I shifted back to the map and the overview of the scene and was surprised that on the map, the lines showed the small little road I had noticed on my way out of that neighborhood. It had been so small I assumed it was a private driveway or a way to reach the Passaic River to drop off a boat to go fishing. Since it was one of the choices I could view from street level, I allowed the computer to follow it. It was also photographed in summer and the greenery barricaded the view down the road, but the previous day there wasn't any house I could see on that block.

I used the touch pad to move forward, and in a flash the image moved all the way to the end of the road. I was looking at the Passaic River, the asphalt lowering into a ramp that went directly into the water. It was clearly a boat launch site and it was obvious that it had been used a great deal.

I used the touchpad to rotate the view to see that there was a house at the end of the road.

My blood went cold.

It was not as large as the structure from the previous night, but it was covered in weathered brown wood shingles.

I moved the view back and forth looking at the building. This was it! The house I had seen in Derrick Johnson's mind. The differences were now clear to me. I had been *so* wrong with the other one.

There was also a tall wooden fence at the back of this house, and I knew it was where the RV containing Lindwall had been hidden.

Delivery…

The buzz hit the back of my brain and made chills go up my spine. This was the place where Lindwall had been waiting for the final parts that would allow him to release the virus from the tanks.

I stopped myself and looked up at the ceiling, trying to gather my thoughts.

"He was waiting there for the delivery," I said aloud to the empty room.

I knew — down to my bones — that we had missed our opportunity.

Whatever Lindwall had been waiting for was already in his possession.

14. BAD TIMING MALADY

"L en, are you sure?" Bill's voice was tense.

"You can look at it yourself on the computer!" I shouted. He had good reason to doubt me after the failed raid, but I knew I was right.

"Calm down, calm down, give me the address again."

"There wasn't a house number on the map," I explained, and gave him the name of the road again. "Are you in the meeting room?"

"No, in my office," Bill admitted. "I figure I can look this up before we involve anyone else."

"Is that wise?"

"Look, Len, the team spent half the night emptying out that trailer park. We had to take people to different towns and seal up that house. It was a long night, and only half the team is even here."

"Okay, sorry. Let me know when you have it," I grumbled.

It took a few minutes, but Bill was able to track down the road, and using the on-line program he was able to get a view from the street level.

"Damn," Bill muttered. "That looks almost exactly like the house we raided last night."

"There are a lot of differences, but you can see why I made the mistake."

"I can."

"Bill, I have a bigger concern. I think Lindwall got the thing he was waiting for, and it could explain why Lanie got so sick last night."

"Why, what do you mean?"

"I think they had some way to release the virus. When they found out she was FBI, they tested it on her."

There was silence on the other end of the phone.

Finally Bill spoke. "Tice is sick, Len. Doctors let us know this morning that he's showing symptoms."

"That fast?" I said, but I had to admit it made sense. If Lanie had been exposed the previous night and ended up unconscious within hours, Tice could easily be manifesting the disease through secondary exposure. The only reason I wasn't sick was because I had been outside. Although I touched her gun, I had been careful not to touch my face or eyes before Tice and I were shoved into the decontamination tent.

Bill exhaled heavily. "Let me get the team on the move. Maybe they haven't had a chance to place the canisters yet."

"Do you know how many there were?" I asked.

"We haven't been sitting on our asses here, Len. The team has been tracking down everything that was used or shipped to that makeshift lab for Stanislaw. He accepted delivery of four metal tanks, about the size they use for oxygen tanks."

"How big?"

"Each one is about three feet long and ten inches in diameter."

"Shit, you can hide something like that almost anywhere."

"We are aware of that as well. I can't see how they could have done anything last night. We had police officers all over the streets of Mountainview, as well as FBI and Homeland Security in plainclothes."

Except during the raid...

"Not during the raid," I said, the psychic flash opening up my mind. "Look Bill, what if Lindwall found out about the raid?"

"How could he know about it?"

I wondered that myself. But if Lanie was FBI and had a handler, someone in that organization could have been leaking information to Lindwall. It could explain why she had to be in deep cover and how she got exposed.

"What if Lindwall somehow found out we were raiding the wrong place, and took advantage of that distraction to have his crew set the tanks with the virus?"

"Look, Len," he sighed. His exhaustion was palpable and I knew how fortunate I was that he still trusted me. "Try to find out what you can, that way you do. I'm going to lead a raid on the address you just gave us."

"Bill, you have to get me out of here. I'm no good to you stuck in here."

"What if you're sick or contagious?"

"We're running out of time—"

"Then let me get moving with the team, Len. I'll do what I can."

He ended the call, and I sat staring at my phone. What had I expected? For him to make one phone call and bail me out?

It was then I heard a knock at my door, and a woman entered. I assumed she was my doctor as she wasn't the nurse I had seen earlier.

She strode in wearing a mask, a paper apron over her scrubs, gloves, a plastic shield, and surgical cap on her head. What was eerie was that her eyes were two different colors, brown and blue, a heterochromia iridum or iridis. I might not have noticed, except her eyes were the only thing I could see.

She looked at the clipboard in her hands. "Hello Mister Wise, I'm Doctor Miller. How are you feeling?"

"Doctor Wise, please. I feel fine, not sick at all. How is Detective Tice?"

"I'm sorry, I am not allowed to divulge patient information."

"I see."

"All of your tests came back negative. I think we might be able to get you out of here."

I sat up and turned to rise from the bed. "Great! If I can get my wheelchair, I will be—"

She raised a hand. "Now, now. When I say out of *here* I mean out of isolation and into a ward. We want to move you to a private room for observation."

"If I'm not a danger to anyone, I need to get out of here. There are people depending on me."

"Oh? How so?" she demanded.

I paused for a moment. I couldn't tell her about the investigation, as I didn't know how much information she had been given. I was sure she knew about the virus, but any other information would have been restricted.

"I work with the police," I attempted lamely.

She looked at her clipboard. "Which explains why you were brought from a scene where a shotgun had been discharged and why you rode in an ambulance with a detective. I can tell you one thing about Detective Tice, he is very sick. You rode to the hospital with him, so you were exposed."

"We were decontaminated at the site," I argued.

She glanced down at her paperwork. "I don't have that information on my report. In fact, what I do have is a lack of background information at all. Perhaps you could tell me what you were doing there last night?"

"That's police business."

"Being in the hospital is medical business. What kind of a doctor are you, anyway?"

"I studied to be a surgeon, and then a psychiatrist."

This caused her to lift one eyebrow. "Really? Well, then you have to appreciate the need for quarantine from a medical perspective, and if you disagree, you should have your head examined."

I nodded at her joke. "Okay, but can I at least get out of this prison cell?"

"I'll get the nurse working on it. We can probably move you tomorrow morning."

"*Tomorrow?*" I repeated, shocked.

"It may surprise you, *Doctor* Wise, but we are dealing with hundreds of patients, and you do not get preferential treatment."

"I understand, Doctor," I said after a moment. She was right, even if it pissed me off.

"Good," she said and made some notes on the clipboard. "I will be off duty, but Doctor Patel will be taking over, if you're okay with foreigners."

This last thing she said caught my attention. "What?"

She sighed. "He's from India, but seems to know what he's doing, not like some people around here."

Like the blacks...

What popped into my head wasn't a buzz in the usual sense. It seemed to be a continuation of her sentence and I heard it in my mind in her voice, as if she spoke it. I thought I should make eye contact and take a peek inside her head, to see if she really felt that way, but she turned away and headed for the door.

"I'll make sure your dinner is brought here, but in the meantime, sir, relax."

She stepped out of the room and closed the door.

"Curiouser and curiouser," I said aloud, trying to understand the glimpse I had received from her mind. I waited, laying my head back. I knew she had to remove the PPE clothing and perhaps change her shoes in the small locker room.

I waited a good ten minutes, then I made sure I put my laptop back in its bag. I grabbed my trusty cobra-headed cane and used it to help me stand. My leg hurt, but not too badly, and I had years of practice using the cane to take the weight off my right leg.

I went to the door and tried the knob, afraid that it was locked, but it turned easily in my hand. I grabbed the backpack from the kneehole under the visitor phone. In the bathroom, I yanked off the hospital gown and pulled the clothing out of the bag. Thank goodness Mrs. Higgins had packed shoes and socks for me as well. She also included a long dark raincoat with a warm lining and a hat. Considering how security was in hospitals these days with cameras everywhere, the hat was probably a good addition. I could use it to block my face on my way out.

I stopped for a moment to take a deep breath. I was about to sneak out of a hospital, and that might be a problem. I closed my eyes and focused my mind. I would need to time this right to get away with it and there was no way I could know what was happening out in the hall. I had to surrender and let my extra senses guide me.

Relaxed and allowing my mind to be blank, I left the backpack in the bathroom and stepped back into the isolation room, the hat in my left hand.

I grabbed my laptop bag and stepped briskly to the door. I took a peek through the visitor window, then went through the door into the outer room and paused. I waited as two nurses walked past, then I stepped into the hall and put the hat on my head, angling it so that it blocked my face as best as possible.

Although I'd been brought up on a private elevator, the main elevators were just down the hall. As I reached the nurses' station, I heard an alarm go off and I froze.

The jig is up.

I heard a male nurse say, "It's Mister Conti in 12 E."

All the other nurses rushed to follow him, leaving only one nurse at the station who was watching the others as they went to help the troubled patient.

I simply limped by the station and went to the elevator.

Danger...

I was standing near the women's rest room. I quickly glimpsed around to see if anyone was looking at me, but the one person at the station was still focused on the group that went to help the patient in distress.

The elevator door opened and I limped in, with my weight still more on the cane than my leg. As the elevator traveled down to the main floor, I relaxed, as I knew it well from numerous times I had been a patient or visited here.

The elevator doors opened and I limped towards the entrance, taking out my cell phone as I went.

"Sir, wait a moment," I heard a deep voice say.

I turned to see a beefy security guard coming around a desk toward me, and my heart leapt to my throat.

He stepped closer and said in a low voice. "Use your cell phone outside, please. It messes with the hospital equipment. Didn't they tell you that?"

"I'm sorry, I forgot," I wheezed.

"Just be careful, sir."

"Th-thank you," I replied and stepped through the door and outside into the cold, dark night.

I was surprised it was night, but I glanced at my watch and it was after 5:40 so it made sense it was dark this early. I hadn't really thought this through. After a moment of indecision, I decided to use the ride share app on my phone to get me back home and to my van.

Then what? I had no resources and no plan.

I needed to find those canisters, and I was the best person to do it.

"Len?" I heard a voice I knew well.

I looked up to see Bill McGee approaching from the parking lot, holding the top of his heavy coat closed against the whipping wind.

"Bill?" I asked. "What are you doing here?"

"I was coming to see you. Christ, should you be walking on that leg?"

"I had to get out."

Bill looked at me sternly, seeming like he was about to ask a question but deciding against it. He shrugged his massive shoulders, and finally said. "My car isn't far, come on."

I appreciated the concern written all over his face.

"I thought you'd be raiding that location I told you about," I said as we walked, steering the conversation away from hospital breakouts and questionable physical abilities.

"I stayed behind this time. But they got out there pretty fast, much faster than last night."

"Was having you along slowing them down?" I joked.

"Probably. It's odd, when I call Gabe Petrie the team moves out pretty fast, but whenever I involve Calvin and Marsh, things take longer."

"Well, they're from Washington. I think things have to be approved by bureaucrats before they can move."

"Maybe, but I was FBI and as I recall, we had a lot of autonomy. I came by to see if I could help you get any insight."

I shook my head. "I haven't tried yet."

"If you're right about the location, you might also be right about the canisters being placed last night."

We reached Bill's car and I got in the passenger side. It was odd for me, as I could actually bend my leg to get in and didn't have to lean sideways so I would fit.

The vehicle was still warm, and I was grateful to sit down. My 'escape' had exhausted me, and the throb in my leg reminded me that I was still not my old self.

"You wouldn't have a wheelchair in your car by any chance?" I asked.

"Didn't think of it," he said and started the car. "How did you manage to get them to release you?"

"I didn't quite get them to release me. My tests came back negative, and I felt it was time."

McGee shook his head. "I'm sure there will be a problem over this. You were in isolation, Len."

"I'm not sick, and we have to find those canisters."

"Okay, swami, where do I go?"

I paused for a moment and considered it. "The most logical place is one of the train stations in town. There are numerous places to hide things and it would have the most impact by infecting commuters."

"Okay, that's a good start," McGee agreed as he started the engine. "With the weather being cold, people will wait inside for the train."

"Which could increase the possibility of inhaling the disease."

Bill backed out of the parking space and aimed the car for the exit. "You know there are four stations in town, right?"

"I do. Try the one on Bloomdale Avenue first. Then we can work our way to the others."

"You got it," he said as he put his credit card in the parking meter so we could exit the lot.

"I'm going into a light trance to see if I get any ideas of where to look."

"You do that," McGee replied.

I closed my eyes and felt the car jostling under me as we drove. I needed to get an idea of where they could have hidden the virus canisters.

More importantly, I had to try to understand how they could have placed them without being noticed.

I thought about Lindwall. I focused on seeing him at the table of the RV with Derrick Johnson and the other man.

I saw a face, the one I had seen on that first night inside the RV.

It was the other guy, and for a moment, I tried to get his name. It was something odd like Gilroy or Gilfried. Then it struck me: Godfrey, who liked to be called God.

Suddenly an image burst into my consciousness. I was walking and looked up to see him, Godfrey Hermann.

This wasn't a vision. Somehow, I had tapped into a memory of someone who had seen Godfrey. I relaxed and tried to focus on the image. I tried to get a sense of where and when this happened.

Although I have had luck with out-of-body experiences, this incident was closer to the theories my mentor, Doctor Kohl, had postulated about how psychic abilities work. I had focused on the men I'd seen with Lindwall, and this allowed me to tap into an active mind that had seen the same face previously.

I had touched someone's memory and was reliving it hours later.

The view I had of Godfrey showed him wearing gray coveralls with a baseball cap pulled down to his eyes. This was unlike the fatigues he had been wearing in my previous vision.

What was frightening for me was that he was pushing a short metal tank on a hand truck.

I noted an embroidered PSEG logo on the front of the coverall right over the breast pocket as he passed by. In Northern New Jersey, PSEG stands for Public Service Electric and Gas. The Newark based company was in control of the electric grid as well as the natural gas pipelines under Mountainview's streets. Seeing a uniformed PSEG service man with a tank on a hand truck wouldn't attract much attention.

In fact, the person whose eyes I watched through thought little of it as Godfrey passed him. Most people would assume he was just doing maintenance.

I focused on my breath and tried to go deeper, seeing if I could tell who had seen Godfrey in that brief moment. I saw a quick flash of a dark blue sleeve, and realized that my host was a Mountainview police officer in uniform.

I tried to zero in on the surroundings. It was a large open space. I could make out large windows, more like showroom windows than household ones. I saw benches around the room for people to sit. This was a train station, and my guess would be the newest one, as the style was modern.

I allowed the images to fade, and pulled myself back to reality. If I was right, then a police officer had seen Godfrey with a canister either last night or today and had just dismissed him.

"Is Bloomdale Station the one they upgraded recently?" I asked aloud, my eyes closed.

"Yes, it's an entirely new building."

"Then that's the one," I confirmed.

"We can be there in a few more minutes. Should I call for backup?"

"I'm not sure."

"You're a big help," McGee mumbled.

"I need to go in to sense if it is hidden in that station."

"You said you were going into a trance. What did you see?"

"Godfrey Hermann in a PSEG uniform, in the train station pushing a tank on a hand truck."

McGee gripped the steering wheel tighter. "That's not good."

"I know," I said, and the feeling of dread within me grew stronger.

15. HIDDEN POISON

We pulled into the parking lot of the Bloomdale station, which was still mostly full of cars for commuters who had yet to return from Manhattan.

Bill jumped out of the car after pulling it into a handicapped space. I used my cane and got out of the car as judiciously as I could.

"Where do I go, where do I look?" Bill demanded.

"I don't know," I said as I limped towards the main door.

"Len, this doesn't help!"

"Bill, I have to get in there and open myself to allow what can come. You know I don't control it."

Bill exhaled heavily as he followed me. "Dammit, I would think by now you could be a little more dependable."

I stopped and turned to face my friend. "It's been a rough week."

"I know," he apologized. "Sorry, I just get frustrated sometimes."

I understood Bill's vexation. I wished that information would come to me in perfect, easy to understand tidbits that I could effortlessly cobble together into accurate information.

It seldom did.

It came to me as it did, sometimes in perfect clarity and sometimes as a vague image that I had to puzzle out.

I was tired, in pain, and fighting my own limitations and fatigue the entire time. I was bolstered by the idea that to give up would result in hundreds, maybe thousands of deaths.

We entered the building and stepped into the large waiting room. It was an open space with tall support columns evenly spaced, and a vaulted ceiling that rose up two floors. I could see a second floor balcony that covered over half the waiting area. On the first floor, there were benches for people to sit and little shops that sold coffee or reading materials. All of it was newly finished, freshly painted and a great example of a modern update of the older stone building.

I stopped and put my hand on one of the substantial supporting columns and closed my eyes.

"Len," McGee fretted. "I didn't know you were so tired."

"I'm not, Bill. I am trying to 'feel' the building and see what it can tell me."

I was grateful he didn't question me. He stood by me silently as I allowed my mind to reach out and sense anything that felt wrong in the superstructure of the train station.

In a sense, a building is like a person. It doesn't have a soul or a mind, but all of the parts of it are interconnected to create the overall structure.

I was searching for anything that didn't fit.

I allowed my mind to glide along steel beams, up and down the length of the building. One moment I was in the lower levels where trash was removed, and then the second floor, at the bar where commuters could grab a coffee or a drink.

Then I *felt* it.

It seemed to glow within my mind's eye. One small place where there was something that was just *wrong*. It didn't belong, and not only did I know it, the building knew it as well.

I opened my eyes and across the waiting room I saw a door with a sign that read "MAINTENANCE."

I lifted my free arm and pointed. "There. That maintenance room, at the far end of the waiting room."

Bill gazed over to where I pointed and squinted. "I see it. Is that where it is?"

"Yes," I replied and then shut my eyes to try to picture the anomaly I had perceived. "It's up high, off the ground, I think. Get on the phone with me to give you instructions."

"Is that necessary?" Bill exclaimed.

This was a good point. Usually any information I told him allowed him to go off and handle a situation. But I could sense... *something*. I thought there might be danger, and I had to be in communication with him to prevent a disaster.

"Yes," I commanded. "Please Bill, it's important."

He pulled his phone from his pocket, annoyed but willing, and dialed my number. I had my phone in my hand before he'd finished. "Okay, stay in constant contact."

Bill nodded and moved forward through the large waiting room. He spoke into the phone as he went. "Once I'm in, where should I look?"

"Not sure. Up, I guess," I said into the phone.

I watched Bill as he moved to the door and he soon closed the distance, the phone still next to his ear. He pulled at the handle, but it didn't budge. "It's locked."

I sighed deeply. "You need to get in there."

"What do you want me to do? Shoot the lock?"

I decided that with commuters on their way through the station that might be a poor choice.

"Can you force it?" I asked.

"I don't think so. It's a steel door and the lock is solid."

"Great. How did Godfrey get in there?" I wondered.

"Len, I have a snap gun in my car. I'll get it."

"A what?" I asked, but I saw Bill was on the move heading back to the unmarked police car in the lot.

"It's a lock-pick gun, and it's pretty handy. Of course, they're illegal for civilians. A pity we don't have your brother here."

Bill was referring to my twin brother, Thomas, a famed Las Vegas magician, who was an expert at picking locks. In fact, his skills with handcuffs had allowed him to rescue Bill on a previous case of mine.

I had provided distraction by getting beaten up.

Bill was back with a small case, and I moved into the waiting area so I could watch him. I plopped myself down on one of the commuter benches to give my leg a rest. Even with the cane taking my weight, it still hurt.

Bill pulled the contraption out of its case. From where I sat, it looked less like a firearm and instead resembled a spring action hand squeeze exerciser more than anything else.

He pulled a flat wire out of the little bag and shoved it into the lock, then pressed the pointed end of the device into the lock and compressed the handle several times. He then rotated the machine and the door opened.

With a glance around the room and then at me, he returned his phone to his ear as he went into the closet and closed the door.

"What does it look like in there?" I asked.

"Small and tight. I'm using the light on my phone to see."

"Anything where a canister could be hidden?"

"There's a locker in front of me, but it's divided into eight little squares. It couldn't be big enough for one of the tanks. You said to look up, but there is nothing on top of the locker."

"Is there a drop ceiling?"

There was a pause, I assumed while Bill moved the light up to look. "There is."

"Can you take a peek into it?"

"Conveniently, there's a ladder in here."

"Seems like someone planned this out."

I heard noises as Bill unfolded the ladder and climbed it.

"I'm raising the ceiling now."

"Carefully, Bill."

"Christ," he cursed.

"What?"

"I'm looking right at it. It looks like it's chained to a metal beam against the wall. Let me see if it—"

Danger…

"Don't touch it Bill," I blurted. "I think it's booby-trapped."

"Why would they do that?"

"I think they want it so that if someone touches it—"

"They get a blast of the virus?"

"You need to call the hazmat team, and shut down this station."

"Len, go outside, wait in the car. I'll make phone calls and see if I can get someone in charge to get here."

"Okay, Bill," I said and rose to move to the door, ending the call as I went. I made it almost to the door when a commuter bumped into me.

"Excuse me," I said, trying to keep myself upright.

I felt a hard metal object push against my side.

"Y'all gonna keep walking, but go the direction I tell ya, got that?"

I glanced back to see the skinny face of Godfrey Hermann next to me. He jabbed me with the barrel of a handgun to accentuate his point.

"Sure, that's fine," I said.

I limped along as best as I could, though I slowed my pace a little to give the impression that I was more injured than I really was.

He guided us toward a van in the middle of the lot.

"I thought you left town, like Lindwall," I said in a low voice.

"Keep walkin'," Godfrey replied and jabbed me again with the gun.

"Some leader you have. He runs off and leaves you to die with the victims."

"Just taking care of loose ends, like you." He reached up and pulled the van passenger door open and looked at me with his large eyes. He had a lazy eye that didn't move with the other. "Shut up and get in."

"Where are you taking me?"

"Lanie said you were a fuckin' psychic, so you tell me. Now, get in or I'll put you in."

I climbed up into the seat.

"Throw the cane into the back," he said and in the darkness of the parking lot, he pulled the gun from his pocket to aim it at me, so I could see it better.

I gently tossed the cane onto the bench seats behind us.

"Give me your phone."

I glanced again at the gun, which seemed to have grown larger, and handed him my cell phone. He took a step back and threw it with an overhand toss toward one of the trash cans.

It clattered as it landed next to the bin.

He slammed the door, lowered the gun out of sight, and quickly went around the front and got into the driver's seat. He immediately started the van. "So, was she right? Y'all some kind of psychic?"

At that moment, the only thought that went through my head was that if I was so good, how come I didn't sense him moving up on me?

"Lanie's sick. She was in a coma the last I heard."

"I know all about that." He faced ahead, shifted into gear, and the van moved toward the exit. "We had to spray her. She was a cop." His jaw became firm. "We're in a war. There'll be casualties."

"This isn't a war, this is an attack. Innocent people will die."

"Shut up, Jew boy," he snapped. "The white man is dyin' cause of forced assimilation, engineered by the Jewish conspiracy to destroy the white race."

Obviously Godfrey was a true believer.

He went on. "I've been following y'all since you snuck outta the hospital. Gotta tell ya, that was pretty slick."

"You saw me leave the hospital?"

He snickered at this. "Yeah, and you led the cop right to the train station and that maintenance room. Makes me think that Lanie was right about you. She said y'all were tryin' to reach into our minds. It figgers you'd be a Jew."

I stared ahead and tried to get my head around what he was saying. He knew I snuck out? How? Then he followed McGee and me to the train station, where he must have decided that I was the one who could locate the canisters.

Which meant I was the biggest threat.

I wanted to keep him talking. "Lindwall was waiting for timers connected to sprayers — what are they, some kind of atomizer?"

"Maybe y'all ain't so smart after all. Those atomizers do more than just go off one time. They release the virus slow, over hours, maybe even days. Maximum exposure."

"You infect the commuters, then they infect other people…"

"And it spreads. And we'll be in Montana until it's all over."

If he was telling me where he was going, he was probably committed to the idea that I was going to be dead.

The view in the van's headlights was becoming more rural as we turned onto country roads. Spending a great deal of time in the more urban part of the state, I often forget why New Jersey is known as "the Garden State." This man was driving me to a secluded location where Lindwall could plant me... permanently.

We drove for about twenty minutes. He kept giving me sidelong glances with a grin on his face. He was enjoying this. I guess murderous racist scum need their amusement wherever they can get it.

We passed a small building with a sign reading "Bill's Luncheonette" and we went up a sharp incline. He then turned right onto a nearly invisible dirt path until we arrived in a gravel parking lot, the stone crunching under our tires.

The headlights of the van lit up a large RV in the lot that had been hidden by the darkness.

This couldn't be good.

Godfrey pulled next to the RV and doused the lights. He got out, and I noted that the interior light had been disabled or removed, as no light came on in his van. He came to my side of the vehicle, threw the door open, and stepped back. I could only see his silhouette, but I was sure he had the gun out and was pointing it at me.

"I need my cane," I said.

"Y'all can limp," he retorted. "Now move it, or I'll just shoot ya out here."

I slid off the seat and landed on the ground on my left leg, using the van to help me as I stumbled along. He backed away as I approached, gesturing with the gun for me to walk ahead of him.

I held onto the RV as we rounded the corner and approached the door.

"Open it," he ordered.

As I did, a light appeared inside. I realized that the windows were covered, but the inside was lit by that flickering oil lamp I had seen in my vision.

I used the rail to pull myself up and onto the first step, with Godfrey behind me.

Suddenly, my mind was filled with an image as reality faded around me, and I saw a hand grasping the rail for the steps, but it wasn't my own.

It was a woman's hand.

I heard a female voice call out, "Joe, what's going on?"

It was the same voice I had heard come from the mobile home last night. Lanie.

Everything was sepia tones around me and I looked up the stairs to see a skinny man standing over me wearing a gas mask and rubber gloves. In slow motion he lifted a small tank, the top was painted green and it wore a decal that read "OXYGEN."

A spray of cold hit me in the face, which made me fall back, coughing.

The man in the gas mask spoke, his voice muffled but the Southern accent made it clear it was Godfrey. "Thought you could fool us? We know you're FBI!"

Then I was running, running back to my car, the bright green one that was nearby, beginning to feel my throat close—

I felt a push on my shoulder and the vision vanished. Godfrey said, "Get in there, dammit."

I went up the stairs, the man in the gas mask and the woman's hand flickering in my memory.

As I reached the top of the steps, seated at the table with the glass tube of the burning lamp in front of him, was Joseph Lindwall.

"Is this the guy, God?" Lindwall demanded.

"Sure is. Saw him lead that detective right to the Bloomdale station, and then to the maintenance room. Heard him on his phone telling the cop that it was booby-trapped and everything."

Lindwall frowned. "So, you're the one that has made me change my plans a few times. Me and God did some research on you. Of course, you would be a Jew."

"Mister Lindwall, you have to stop this," I attempted. "People will die, even white people—"

"Shut up and sit down," Lindwall said before Godfrey roughly pushed me into a chair. He stared across the table at me. "Lanie was a big help to me. She told me a lot about you."

I found that interesting as I had never even met the woman.

He leaned back in the chair. "Pity she was FBI. We had no choice but to take her out."

"How did you find out she was an agent?" I asked.

Godfrey slapped the back of my head. "We ask the questions, Jew boy."

This made Lindwall's smile grow. "I heard she almost took you out with a shotgun."

Both Lindwall and Godfrey chuckled at this.

"She thought it was you," I replied, expecting another slap from Godfrey.

Lindwall slammed his fist on the table, the look of amusement gone. "You think I don't know that? She was a fighter, I'll give her that much."

"If there is an antidote—"

This made him smile in a wolfish grin. "The only cure is distance. Lanie went back to that mobile park, and I had hoped she'd infect as many people as she could. But then you showed up, and her ex, the cop. That bunch from Homeland evacuated the place and shut down any risk of spreading the virus."

I frowned at this. "How did you know?"

"Godfrey was watching."

It was at this point I realized that any entreaties I might attempt would be a waste of time. There was only "the cause" and all other human emotions were gone.

He went on. "I need distance. The original plan was that Lanie was going to ride with us, get us safely out of the state. Since she's no longer able to, I decided that it would be fitting if you give us the best way out."

I frowned. "I don't understand."

"If you can do the stuff she said you can, then I need you to pick the routes I should take. You're gonna ride with us."

"Why would I do that?" I sassed him.

Godfrey spoke up. "Because we'll kill you if you don't."

"You're going to kill me anyway," I responded, and the realization of that felt heavy on my shoulders.

"But we can kill you quick… or slow," Godfrey said with his wicked grin again. "I like to do it slow."

I considered it. This might just give me a way to lead Lindwall right into a police checkpoint. He'd shoot me, but at least the pair of them would be stopped.

Headlights flashed outside the window as another vehicle pulled up. I couldn't see what it was through the closed curtains, but Lindwall stood.

"I've arranged an incentive, Jew boy, in case you had any doubts."

I heard someone yell outside and I froze as I recognized the voice.

Jyanette.

The door to the RV opened and Jyanette was pushed in, falling up the steps. There in the open doorway stood Agent John Marsh.

Suddenly it was clear to me and I was plunged into another vision.

I could see Lanie as she drove her car away from here after being struck with the gas that contained the virus. She spoke on her phone to this man, telling him she'd been sprayed, and he advised her to go back to the mobile home park. He promised a team of men in hazmat suits would meet her there. I saw Marsh as he phoned Lindwall and told him he needed to move to checkpoint C until it was safe to leave.

Marsh had been Lanie's controller, but gifted with her own psychic abilities, she hadn't made the connection that Marsh worked with Lindwall, and was part of the insane plan all along.

It must have taken Marsh years of hiding his true feelings to rise in the ranks within the FBI, but he had done it. Like Lindwall, Marsh was a true believer.

I blinked, clearing my mind and lurched out of my chair toward Jyanette. With my bad right leg, I almost fell on top of her.

"Len?" she gasped, and I held her, moving in front of her protectively.

"She the one?" Lindwall barked.

"Yeah," Marsh explained, looking like he was bored by the whole thing. "I heard from Calvin that she and the Jew used to be hot and heavy."

"At least your partner dates his own kind," Godfrey said, his eyes running up and down Jyanette's body in such a lascivious way, that I wanted to punch him.

"He isn't my partner, he was assigned to me," Marsh said. "And I don't like the way he's been watching me. I think he suspects something."

"What about her phone and purse?" Lindwall asked.

"I've got them in the car. I'll take them back to MPD. By the time they start to look for her, all they'll find is the purse."

"Good. When do you leave town?"

"Right after I drop off the purse. I can't risk staying any longer with Calvin breathing down my neck."

"I told you the coon would be nothing but trouble."

"Yeah, he's smarter than I thought, so it's time to leave. I heard over the radio that they found that one canister in the Bloomdale Station, and they're working on it right now."

"Did they get that radar equipment you told me about?" Lindwall asked.

"Setting it up even now. It was sent in a sealed box, so I wasn't able to sabotage it, what with Calvin watching my every move. But, even with that, I doubt they'll find the other canisters fast enough."

"We'll move ahead with the plan, and meet up at the rendezvous."

Marsh nodded and with a look of disgust at me, walked down the steps and out of the vehicle.

Lindwall and Hermann looked over at me, with Jyanette behind me. She wasn't cowering, but I still wanted to put something between these awful men and my love.

"So, your name is Wise, right?" Lindwall demanded.

"Leonard Wise," I muttered.

"Okay, Lenny. I'm going to give you some maps. You get us a route out of New Jersey. If you make any mistakes, God here is gonna cut off one of your lady's fingers."

Godfrey, as if on cue, pulled a switchblade from his pocket and extended the blade so it gleamed in the firelight. He smiled at the cutting edge.

Lindwall went on. "If we run into a roadblock or a police stop, I'll shoot her before I shoot you. And if you do anything I don't like, God will take her into the back and show the lady a few things he enjoys, which I hear are pretty rough on the ladies he shares them with."

I felt my stomach twist, hurting worse than my leg at that moment.

Lindwall reached into his pocket and pulled out a pair of handcuffs, which he tossed underhand to me. "Cuff her. Hands in the front in case God has to remove any fingers."

I turned to face Jyanette and saw the panic in her eyes. I opened the cuffs and carefully put the shackles around each of her wrists. The chain on the cuffs was longer than in a standard pair, and I assumed it was so they could be wrapped around a solid object.

I met her eyes.

I'm so sorry…

Surprise made her eyes widen. She had heard my voice in her head as I was projecting the thought to her. When we dated, I didn't ever push my way into her mind, but at this moment I needed her to know how I felt.

I love you…

"Good enough," Lindwall warned. He pushed the maps over the table top and I sat with the papers out in front of me.

Lindwall gestured to Jyanette. "Now, Missy you sit right here next to God and me, and we can keep an eye on you in case your boyfriend gets any ideas."

Lindwall sat across from me, and Jyanette slid in next to him. Godfrey, with that same malevolent grin, pulled in next to her and started to play with his switchblade, opening and closing it again and again.

---

16. TRAVEL SICKNESS

I poured over the maps, drawing lines as I focused on a route that would get us out of New Jersey and into Pennsylvania. Lindwall said he wanted to use back roads until we were out of the state. I ran my fingers over the different westbound routes, trying to allow my extra senses to find the clear path.

It was cold in the RV, but I was sweating and my leg was throbbing, which was an unneeded distraction.

We were near a town called Chester, and I was led to a route that would take the RV through Long Valley and onto Route 57 in Hackettstown. From there he could follow secondary roads until we hit Easton, Pennsylvania. From that location, he had the choice to stay on side roads or move to the major highways very easily.

Lindwall looked at the map and the lines I had drawn and nodded. "This will work." He looked over at Godfrey. "Cuff him to the chair."

"Wait, I did what you wanted," I bleated, hating to sound so pathetic.

Godfrey pulled out another pair of handcuffs with a shorter chain, and deftly snapped my wrist to the solid wood arm of the chair.

"I want to make sure you don't try anything while I'm driving," Lindwall sneered. With the map in his hand, he shoved Jyanette so she slid out from behind the table and rose to her feet, where Godfrey caught her by her shoulders.

She flinched at his touch.

Lindwall stood, lifted the oil lamp by the base, and headed toward the front of the RV.

I glanced back to Jyanette. Only her eyes and Godfrey's could be seen in the dim light. Lindwall started the overlarge machine. I heard the roar of the powerful engine as it came to life.

He carefully blew out the oil lamp and placed it on the floor in front of the passenger seat. He also took out a handgun from a waist pack and placed it on the console between the two seats.

Godfrey still held Jyanette, and caressed her shoulders. Her revulsion was palpable.

He pushed her to the padded bench she'd been sitting on before and Jyanette slid away from him as the big vehicle began to move.

"Jew boy, be careful on that chair," Godfrey told me. "It ain't built in, and y'all might fall over."

He kicked the side of it, making it rock.

"That's very considerate of you," I fumed.

He held up his knife and extended the blade again. "I just want to know where you are, that's all."

He slid closer to Jyanette, and when she attempted to move away, he reached around her and pulled her closer to him. "Don't leave, honey. Been a while since I had me a black bitch."

He glared at me and smiled again, as if to say, "What are you going to do about it?"

The big vehicle pulled onto the main road, and we were at the top of the hill. Having seen the topography of the map, I knew that for the first part of the journey we'd be going up and down a lot of hills, which this heavy machine might have a bit of trouble with. It wouldn't smooth out until we hit the center of town, which was at least ten miles away.

We drove on, Godfrey holding onto Jyanette possessively, as I seethed. I fought to calm my raging thoughts enough to try to find a way out of this mess. I'd been trained in the martial art of Aikido, but with my leg unable to really support my weight and my hand cuffed to the chair, I couldn't think of any way I could overpower Godfrey, or Lindwall.

Godfrey was getting more aggressive with Jyanette, reaching around and cupping one of her breasts. She struggled to pull away, her face twisted with fear and disgust.

This only made him smile. "I like it when a girl fights," he goaded her. "Makes it more fun to take what I want."

He pulled her close and pinched her nipple. She shrieked in outrage.

Godfrey stood up, swaying as the vehicle moved. "Hey, Joe, I think me and the bitch need some alone time," he yelled over the roar of the RV.

"Just don't kill her," Lindwall called back, his eyes on the road. "We might need her later."

"You get the sloppy seconds," Godfrey claimed, and grabbed Jyanette's arm to yank her to her feet.

"You can't," I cried. "I did what you asked—"

"Calm down, Jew boy," Godfrey snarled. "We're just gonna have us a little fun."

I tried to rise to my feet, but Godfrey just pushed me back and slapped my face, hard. I looked up at Jyanette, panting with rage as my face burned where he'd struck me.

"You just sit there like a good boy," Godfrey told me. "I'm gonna show Missy what it's like to be with a *real* man."

He turned away and pushed Jyanette in front of him, giving her rear end a hard smack. Jyanette screamed, trying to twist away from him.

"Good, you're a screamer," Godfrey said. "I like screamers."

I watched as he pushed her into the back room. I couldn't see much, but I did see the corner of a bed in the room. Godfrey slid the accordion door closed.

I glanced up at Lindwall, who was driving us over another hill, and I shuddered at the noises from the back room. There was the sound of cloth being ripped and a shriek from Jyanette, followed by garbled shouts from Godfrey.

I had to do something! I used both hands to pull on the cuff on my wrist. The arm of the chair was quite solid, but I bore down as the metal bracelet cut into my flesh and I gasped from the exertion.

I felt it move a little and redoubled my efforts. The wooden arm creaked and groaned, and then it lifted. It came loose all at once and almost clocked me in the face. I slid the cuff off the end of the chair arm, and slid over to the bench that surrounded two sides of the table, gasping from exertion.

There was an ominous silence from the back room, and I grabbed the chair arm to pull it free completely. It was the only weapon I had, but at least I had something.

Suddenly blue and red flashing lights strobed through the windshield ahead of us.

Down the street was a roadblock shutting the road off completely. There had to be at least ten police cars blocking the path, making it impossible to ram through even with the overlarge vehicle.

Lindwall lurched the vehicle to a stop, threw it into park, and grabbed the handgun as he moved back to me, fury in his eyes.

"You tricked me, you fuckin' Kike," he bellowed. "But you're gonna see your black bitch die before I kill you."

I held the arm from the chair low and out of sight as he moved past me and toward the closed accordion door. I was grateful that he didn't realize I had moved from the chair.

"God, bring her out here," Lindwall yelled. "I don't care if she's naked. I'm gonna shoot the bitch."

All I could see was his back, his body filling the small passageway. Lindwall held the gun aimed up at the ceiling as he yanked open the folding door.

Lindwall made a strange noise and staggered backward. He turned slowly, revealing the hilt of Godfrey's switch blade knife sticking out of his stomach. Lindwall had a look of shock on his face, but as soon as he saw me, he gasped and pointed the pistol at me.

Leaping up with the little strength I had left, I used the piece of furniture as a club and smashed his hand in an upward arc, shoving the gun up at the roof as it exploded.

I heard Jyanette scream from behind us.

I pulled back and smashed the broken chair arm right into Lindwall's disgusting face. The gun flew from his fingers as he went down.

The door of the RV was yanked open and a dark shape surged in. The flashlight in his hand blinded me moments after seeing the gun he held in front of him.

"Hands up where I can see them," the man yelled. I recognized the voice of Agent Marcus Calvin.

I dropped the wooden implement and raised my hands. Lindwall had landed on his back with the knife still jammed in his gut. I could see his chest rise and fall, drawing breath.

"The perp's down," I said. "There's another in the back."

Marcus pointed the light at the back of the RV as a uniformed police officer followed him.

With her handcuffed arms raised, Jyanette moved up the hall from the back. The sleeve of her blouse was ripped and hung loosely down at her side.

"The other perp is dead," she said wearily. Her hair had come loose from its bun, hanging in limp strands over her face. Her skirt was intact, but there was a large red blood stain in the middle of it.

"Jyanette," I gasped. "You're bleeding."

"I'm fine," she said, breathing hard as well, her teeth clenched. "It's from Lindwall when I stabbed him."

I wanted to go to her, take her in my arms. However, Marcus Calvin moved to her and enveloped her in a hug.

Calvin pulled back to look at her. "What happened?"

"Asshole tried to rape me," Jyanette reported, a seething anger in her tone. "I acted like he was in charge, got the handcuff chain around his neck, and choked the shit out of him."

The policemen, who had moved past Jyanette and Marcus, stuck his head out from the bedroom.

"He's still breathing," the policeman yelled from the back.

"That's a pity," Jyanette replied, then turned to Marcus. "How on earth did you find us?"

"I've been trailing you since Mountainview. I was in the parking lot at MPD when I saw you and Marsh get into his car and drive away. I've been suspicious of Marsh because he'd been acting oddly, not following protocol. Since he didn't let me know where he was going, I followed you. When he pulled in that lot and I saw the RV, I hid until he left. When the RV started to move I called the police to order the roadblock."

"You've saved our lives," I said.

Calvin looked down at Lindwall on the floor. "Looks like you were doing fine." He raised his head and looked at Jyanette. "We have to get you to a hospital."

"I'm fine," Jyanette said and gestured at her bloody blouse. "This is from the perp."

Calvin then looked at me and frowned. "Aren't you supposed to be isolated in a hospital?"

Jyanette met my eyes. "Len?"

I was still recovering from the exertion and the pain in my leg and I slid down into the padded bench. "That doesn't matter. We have to get back to Mountainview and find those other canisters."

Unfortunately, none of this could be done quickly. Jyanette and I were taken out of the RV to wait outside in the cold, as Calvin called out to the police to get an ambulance. Jyanette explained to Calvin that his partner had abducted her, and he moved away to make phone calls, I assumed to catch Marsh before he could get away.

As we waited for an ambulance for the two injured assailants, Jyanette and I stood side by side shivering in the cold. I leaned my back against the RV for support, doing my best to take the weight off my right leg.

A cop came by as we waited and offered both of us coffee, and even suggested a bit of 'cheer' to help on this cold night. Jyanette got hers with the proffered alcohol, but I just had the coffee black.

I had to admit, after almost dying, alcohol sounded really good. But I knew I needed my abilities, as well as the sobriety I had fought so hard to achieve.

Jyanette watched me. "Leg still hurt?"

I grimaced. "Yeah."

We stood there in embarrassed silence, sipping steaming coffee and watching the team move the unconscious men out of the RV.

"How did Marsh get you?" I asked.

She rubbed her wrists, switching the styrofoam cup from hand to hand. When we'd gotten out of the RV, a uniformed officer had used a standard key to remove both of our restraints.

"He told me he had a lead and said I might be a help to offer an informant immunity." She shrugged. "I didn't think anything of it until he drove out to the RV and grabbed my purse. Then he yanked me out of the car and pushed me to the door."

A pair of ambulances pulled up, lights flashing and everyone rushing around us. The roadblock had been formed by the Chester Township Police, thanks to Agent Calvin. It was now breaking up, and men were on the street guiding traffic around the large vehicle.

"You spoke in my head," Jyanette remarked.

"Yeah." Insufficient, but it was all I could manage.

"You never did that with me before."

"It was a desperate circumstance."

"Did you mean it?" she asked.

"What do you think?" I said and met her eyes.

"That's what was strange. I heard the words, but I *felt* your emotions, shared your feelings. I've never experienced anything like that before."

We fell back into silence.

I wanted to say so much. I wanted to tell her that I adored her, that she was the light in my life, and a hundred other things, but to what point? She knew how I felt, now more than ever. She had not only saved her own life, but by stabbing Lindwall had probably saved mine as well.

Calvin approached us. "Doc, you think you can find those other canisters?"

"Yes," I affirmed.

"Then let's head back to Mountainview," Calvin stated. "McGee told me that you were right, the one he found at the train station was booby-trapped, but the hazmat guys defused it. They also got a chance to examine the timer built into the atomizer."

Jyanette stepped closer to Calvin. "Do they know when they were programmed to start releasing the virus?"

"They sure do," Calvin intoned. "Eight AM tomorrow morning."

17. MISPLACED INDISPOSITION

The ride back to Mountainview was pretty frightening, huddled in the back seat of Calvin's government car. The lights flashed and the siren blared and we must have been doing a hundred over roads where I wouldn't risk going forty.

As we rocketed over hill and dale, with me being thrown around in the back, Jyanette turned to face me from the passenger seat. "Any ideas?"

"I haven't had a chance to... do what I do," I replied as the car bounced again. "Are there any other places where commuters would congregate?"

It was Calvin who spoke. "When I called the team about Marsh, they said the other train stations had been evacuated and searched with radar."

"Radar?" I replied. "Marsh said something about that."

Calvin went on. "It's a new device, first developed for use in the wars in Iraq and Afghanistan. It's basically a handheld sensor that sends radar signals through walls."

"Any luck?"

"They found a second canister at the Lackawanna Train Station downtown."

I sat back in my seat and sighed. Two down. The team had sprung into action even after my abduction. McGee was sure to have worried about me once I stopped answering my phone, but he would still focus on the job. Searching the other train stations in town was the next logical choice.

Bus...

I felt the buzz, as much as heard it.

"Any other transportation stations?" I asked. "I know there's a Greyhound bus terminal."

"That's what that profiler, Doctor Yearling, thought," Calvin said. "The team was planning to search it when I called."

"The Greyhound terminal in Mountainview is small," Jyanette added. "But the one in Newark is a huge hub."

"A part of the team could go to Newark once they go through the terminal in Mountainview," Calvin agreed.

This seemed like the choice Lindwall and the Faction would select. Somewhere they could infect a large number of people who would spread it out into the world in a way that would be hard to trace.

Yet, I was sure it was wrong.

A memory or a vision appeared in my mind as I bounced about in the seat. A tall, two-story building with overlarge garage doors and windows that faced the street.

I spoke up. "Don't we have a large private bus company in Mountainview? One that does charters?"

Jyanette sighed. "I'd google it, but I don't have my phone."

Calvin reached into his pocket, pulled a smart phone, and handed it over to Jyanette. He told her the numbers of the passcode, and she opened it to use the internet browser.

After a few minutes, she spoke up. "I found the DeWitt Bus Company. Get this, its offices and main terminal are in Mountainview."

"Take us there," I suggested.

"But the hazmat team is heading for the Greyhound office," Calvin said.

"I think we need to be at the DeWitt terminal," I insisted. "Besides, if we look in more than one place it will increase the odds that we'll find something."

I was vaguely familiar with the DeWitt Bus Company. They had started with horse-drawn carriages in the 1870s and then moved into motor buses when the nineteenth century became the twentieth. They did a lot of custom excursions to casinos and private events as well as a few commuter routes — with several that went into New York City.

The Greyhound Bus Terminal was for people going across the state or across the country, but a local commuter business would increase the possibility of infection and spread.

Jyanette was still looking at the phone. "I think Len's right. I'll pull up your map app and get directions."

"Okay. I'll get on the radio and let everyone know what we're doing."

It only took Jyanette a moment to input our destination and she slipped the phone into a holder on the dashboard.

A female voice began to tell us our turns and Calvin slowed to a reasonable speed. He also shut off the siren, leaving only the flashing lights.

As we drove, Calvin used the microphone of the onboard radio to announce where we were going and keep the team informed.

Once he finished, the only voice was his phone giving us directions. "Your destination is on the left ahead."

Calvin slid the car into the large parking lot and threw it into park. We were in front of the huge building I had seen in my mind. It had been meticulously preserved, a brick building with a style from the early 1900s that encompassed an entire small city block. It was red brick with yellow brick added for decoration and the walls designed into recessed squares. Functionally, one half of the building was the garage where the buses were repaired and met the passengers. The other half of the building was a large waiting room and ticket booths.

A perfect place to release the virus.

Jyanette turned to Calvin. "Who's Vanessa?"

"What?"

"Vanessa," Jyanette said sweetly, with a touch of iron in her voice. "I saw on your phone that she keeps sending you messages."

"She's a… friend," Calvin stammered.

As much as I enjoyed seeing Calvin in the hot seat, I knew we had to get moving. We'd spent a good amount of time waiting around in the cold once the RV had been stopped, and it was already after nine pm.

"We have to go," I stated as I opened my door and rose shakily to my feet.

Jyanette got out of the car and looked at Calvin coolly. "I'll want to hear all about Vanessa later."

We headed toward the building, and I got all of two steps before I almost collapsed and fell against the SUV.

"Len?" Jyanette looked to me, her eyes wide.

"My… leg," I said through gritted teeth.

"I got this," Calvin said, and took off in a run toward the building, as Jyanette helped me to my feet.

"I hate for you to see me like this," I grunted.

"Shut up or I'll break your other leg," she told me as she took my right arm on her shoulder and helped me forward.

Calvin came running back with a folded wheelchair. It was covered in blue vinyl and looked like it had been made in the 1940s, but I was grateful.

"They have these in the bus station, in case of emergency," Calvin explained. "I think this counts."

I sat down and lifted my sore leg onto the metal footrest. Calvin began to push me, and Jyanette walked alongside.

"Where are we going?" Jyanette asked.

"I'm not sure," I shrugged. It was all I could offer.

"That's not good enough, Len," Jyanette chided me.

The people I work with, except maybe McGee, always seem to expect me to pull miracles out of my hat. They don't understand how distractions and exhaustion can affect what I do. The price of my success in previous cases was that people were shocked when I couldn't deliver at the very moment it was wanted or needed.

We got into the building, and Calvin said, "Okay, I'm going to speak to someone in charge in case we need to evacuate."

I nodded. "I'll try to see if it really is here."

Calvin headed off toward the ticket counter of the large building. The waiting room wasn't very full, just a few people sitting around. One guy looked like he was homeless and had come into the terminal just to stay warm. He wore a long, dirty coat, had a scraggily beard, and there was an old paper bag on the seat next to him.

Jyanette leaned forward and whispered into my ear. "Are you getting anything?"

"Yeah, a headache," I responded. "Give me a minute."

I closed my eyes and focused on my surroundings, trying to sense or feel if there indeed was a canister here, and if so where?

In my mind, I saw the homeless guy coming towards us, and then he was replaced by a glowing blue orb. A second glowing orb floated a few feet away, only it had a tawny color to its luminescence.

Danger…

The buzz struck me and I forced open my eyes, but the scene was the same as when I had closed them. The only person who was in a different place was Agent Calvin, talking to a supervisor over in the ticket office.

"Do you know where it is?" Jyanette encouraged.

I shook my head. "I'm getting strange impressions. It doesn't seem to make—"

I stopped talking as my eye went to a grate in the wall. It was large and had a filter blocking the view. Somehow, I knew it ran from the parking garage to the waiting room, a leftover from when this building was constructed in the early part of the last century. No one thought anything about bus fumes coming through to the waiting room in those innocent times. The air filter was a modern addition that would keep the bus exhaust out — but not a virus.

It was the perfect hiding place, as the filter would block anyone from seeing a canister hidden up there.

"Len, what do you have, what are you seeing?"

"The grate on the wall," I whispered to her and pointed at it.

"Is that where it is?" she hissed back.

"I think so... I don't know... there's danger around it," I told her.

She looked down at me in the chair. "Danger? You mean a booby-trap, like the one in the train station?"

I shook my head. "No, this danger is more immediate. Can you push me closer?"

"Is that a good idea?"

"None of this is a good idea, Jyanette."

She grinned a little at this, and then began to push the wheelchair in the direction of the grate. Doing so, we went by the homeless guy who appeared to be reading a magazine as we passed. I glanced sidelong at him, and saw him sneak a look at us as we moved toward the wall.

When we were about ten feet from the grate, I raised my hand to stop her, and gestured for her to bend closer.

"The homeless guy, do you see him?"

"Yeah, he's watching us."

"He might be guarding the canister."

"How do you know? Psychic flash?"

"No," I explained, "sense of smell."

"What?"

"He looks like a homeless guy, but he doesn't smell like one. It's all an act."

Jyanette rose up to her full height, keeping the man in her peripheral vision as she did so.

Suddenly, the main lights went off as an alarm sounded and emergency lights flashed on, but only near the doors, leaving us in a darkened area.

Jyanette leaned in. "I guess a fire alarm is one way to empty a building."

Danger...

I hardly needed the warning and yelled out, "Jyanette, look out."

The phony homeless man had extracted a large hunting knife from his paper sack and was rushing toward us.

I tried to think of what to do. I was stuck in the chair without my trusty cobra-headed cane, which can be a formidable weapon when necessary.

Jyanette pushed my chair away, and in a surprising move, leapt over a bench. Using her hands as if on a gymnastic pommel horse, she flew over it, and when the man jumped for her, he fell onto the heavy wooden bench. With the bench between them, he rose up and Jyanette struck him in the eye with a blow that looked quite painful.

I rolled up behind him, and with a roar, slammed into the back of his legs with the wheelchair. He fell into my lap and I grabbed the hand with the knife. He yelled incoherently and fought like a madman, with a grip of iron on the knife.

A large metal trash can smashed down on his hand and the knife went flying. I looked up to see Jyanette swing the metal contrivance and I leaned back as she smashed it against our attacker's head.

The man crumpled to the ground without any further complications. I wheeled back from him and retrieved the fallen knife as Jyanette put down the metal container.

She was breathing hard and I approached carefully. "Are you all right?"

"I am now," she gasped.

"Have you been taking self-defense classes or something?"

She turned her eyes to me. "Every week since I left NJ."

"Remind me not to piss you off."

Calvin ran up and saw the fallen man. Although the attack had been frightening, it literally only lasted a minute at the most.

"What happened?" Calvin asked and looked down at the fallen man.

"Cuff him, he's one of Lindwall's men," Jyanette ordered.

"He is?" Calvin replied, then fell to one knee and neatly flipped the moaning man over and put handcuffs on his wrists.

"The canister is in that grate on the wall," I said and pointed at the metal plate. "Not sure how they did it—"

"Turns out the terminal closes at midnight," Calvin explained. "If this guy is part of their team, maybe he did it, or he let somebody in who did."

"Wouldn't they have seen him here when they shut down last night?" Jyanette asked.

"He could have hidden in the men's room until the late crew was gone," Calvin said. "The supervisor told me that the morning crew said he was here when they got in. I was about to question him."

"Can you get the hazmat team over here?" I asked.

"I already called them, and they told us to wait outside," Calvin explained, as he pulled our assailant to his feet.

"Good," Jyanette said fixing a cold stare at Calvin. "While we wait, you can tell me all about Vanessa."

At that moment, I actually felt sorry for the FBI man.

But only a little.

18. CONCEALED ROT

Calvin stayed with the prisoner until the police and hazmat team arrived, and then he and Jyanette went back to his government-issued car for their discussion.

I would have loved to hear that conversation, but I was, once again, literally out in the cold. For a brief moment, I considered using astral projection to place my mind within their car to listen, but that would have been cheating.

Besides, I was tired, and there was still one more canister to locate. I had no way of knowing where it was, or even where to start looking.

"Len, what are you doing out here in the cold?" a booming voice asked.

I looked up to see McGee looming over me. He got behind me and pushed the wheelchair into the parking lot towards his unmarked police car.

"Come on, let's get you into the car for some warmth. We can wait there."

"Thanks," I said, too tired to argue.

He pulled open the trunk and held up an object. "I was able to get this back for you."

It was my cobra-headed cane.

I sighed as I used it to get myself to my feet. "This would have come in handy a little while ago."

"I got it when they towed Godfrey Herman's van to impound. I heard you ran into some trouble here at the bus station. Did your Aikido work help?"

"Not much. It was Jyanette the Terminator who stopped him."

"Jyanette?"

"Yeah, she took him down with a trash can."

Bill opened the passenger door for me and helped me in. "That brings a whole new meaning to 'taking out the trash'."

"If you're going to get punny, I'll just sit out in the cold."

I got myself in and Bill went to the driver's side and started the car up, blasting the heat at my feet. It felt wonderful.

I put my head back and closed my eyes.

"So, I'm looking in the maintenance room at the train station, phoning the hazmat team, and all at once you're gone."

"Godfrey Hermann suggested I go with him, and his gun made it a persuasive argument," I said without lifting my head or opening my eyes.

"Next thing I know, you're pulled over at a roadblock and you've captured Joseph Lindwall."

"To be honest, he captured me. Once again, Jyanette got us out of it. I knew she was a fighter, but tonight, she was a tigress. I'd be dead if it weren't for her."

"How did they capture her?"

"Agent Marsh is a member of the Faction. He took her with a bullshit story about speaking with an informant."

"Really?" McGee replied, his tone suggesting that he was genuinely surprised by this revelation. "I know that Marsh left about 5:30, without a word to anyone. No one has seen him since."

"He's on the run."

Bill's phone rang and he answered it. I just sat there, enjoying the heat. I knew I had to find that last canister, and I was planning to slip into a light trance.

As I focused, an odd image came to me: Godfrey on a ladder putting the cylinder in the space above him. He was in the garage section of the bus station, dark buses nearby, his path lit by a short figure on the ground with a flashlight. Next to the ladder was our fake homeless guy, holding the air filter, the metal grate near his feet.

As Godfrey set the tank and activated the timer, the bearded man handed up the filter. Finally, he lifted the metal grate, and Godfrey used a screwdriver to put it in place.

"Is it set?" a female voice asked. The voice was familiar, but I couldn't trace it. It wasn't Lanie, because at this point she was either in her trailer or the hospital.

"Ready to go," Godfrey said as he descended the ladder.

The woman with the flashlight lit the way, but she was clothed in shadows and I couldn't get a glimpse of her face at all.

The scene faded, then there it was again — a black space with a blue orb floating in it. Then a second, darker orb appeared a few feet from it, shining in their own radiance before they both faded away.

Although this vision took several minutes in real time, it was merely seconds within my head.

"Got it," Bill said as he ended the call. "You were right, Len. The canister was behind that grate, hidden by the air filter. If it had started to release the virus it would have infected both the waiting room and the depot. The buses themselves might have spread the virus from people touching the outside of the bus, loading luggage or stepping in."

I nodded. "The team is going to need to sanitize the entire station. That was another canister planted by Godfrey, and there was a woman helping him and our homeless guy."

"A woman? Did you see her?"

"No, but her voice was familiar."

"Do you think there was any kind of exposure? I mean, you and Jyanette were in there," Bill worried.

"I don't think there was a release of the virus."

"The hazmat team is going to set up a decontamination site here, like at the mobile home park. Should you go through decontamination again? Maybe we should take you to the hospital and have you checked out."

Hospital…

The buzz slipped through my mind. Was Bill right, and I needed to go to the hospital? Would they take me there against my will again? It was the last place I felt I needed to be.

"Bill, if I'm in the hospital, we can't locate the final canister. You need me."

"Okay, tough guy. Where do we look?"

I leaned my head back again. "I don't know. I keep getting a vision of a pair of glowing globes."

"Len it's half-past ten, and that final canister is going to start pumping out poison at eight AM. Maybe sooner if any one of Lindwall's group is still in the area to set it off."

"I know, I know," I lamented. "Let me try again."

"Okay, stay in the car, stay warm. I need to go talk to Gabe Petrie and the hazmat team commander."

"No problem there."

Bill got out of the car and I slumped in the seat. There was a knock on the window, and I turned to see Jyanette. I pointed my thumb at the back seat and hit the lock to open the door.

She got in, annoyance written on her face.

"How did it go with Agent Calvin?"

"He's an asshole."

I couldn't fight the smile.

"Don't be smug, or I'll start calling you one as well."

I controlled myself. "So, who's Vanessa?"

"His other girlfriend," she complained. "He gave some lame-ass excuse about how we had just started dating, and he had to keep his options open, and the usual man-shit you guys come up with."

"You never got that from me."

"Yeah? Well, are you pulling that garbage on Kate?"

"Kate's the one who established our relationship as casual. She only became possessive when she saw me looking at you."

"Probably because every time you gape at me, you look like a wounded puppy," she snapped.

"I didn't think you noticed."

"I noticed and it's about as sexy as a wet washcloth. Cut it out."

There was a pause, and I finally said, "You think I'm sexy?"

"Really? *That's* what you got from that?"

"Jyanette, I don't know what I'm supposed to do, or how to act around you. You know how I feel."

Now it was her turn to be silent. "Yes, I do. After tonight, I understand that more than I ever could before."

"So, what should we do?"

"Find the last canister."

"But then you'll be headed back to Washington."

"I promise we'll talk before I do."

The conversation died again, as I had run out of words.

"So instead of us sitting here not talking," she attempted, "do that voodoo thing of yours."

"I can't," I said. "I'm tired, and I'm blocked. I keep seeing the same image over and over. I need a way to get through whatever's stopping me."

Jyanette considered this. "Is there anything you can do? Can anyone help?"

I shrugged. "Kate has used hypnosis on me in the past."

"She was at MPD but that was hours ago, before Marsh abducted me. Let me ask Bill if she's still there, and he can drive us over."

I nodded, and Jyanette got out of the car and headed off toward where Bill was standing.

I watched her go. It seemed like all I had done since September was to watch her go.

A few short minutes later we were pulling into the MPD lot, McGee and I in front and Jyanette riding in the back of Bill's unmarked car.

We had left the borrowed wheelchair at the bus station, and I used my trusty cane to get me up and out of the car with Jyanette's help.

"It's so weird for you to be the one who needs rescuing," Jyanette told me as we walked slowly toward the back door of MPD.

"You've done it several times tonight," I replied. "This is going to ruin my 'man of action' reputation."

"It would hold up better if you didn't lead with your glass jaw," she explained.

Bill, bless him, had run ahead of us and now came back pushing my wheelchair.

"How did you get that?" I wondered.

"When you and Tice were taken to the hospital, they delivered the wheelchair here, all disinfected. Come on, have a seat."

He pushed me the rest of the way.

Kate met us at the door. She took one look at me and Jyanette, and something seemed to click in her mind.

"I'm going to work with Len, *alone*," Kate said. "Push him into one of the bunk rooms."

"The bunk rooms?" Jyanette repeated.

"Look around," Kate huffed. "The place is overrun with federal agents, especially since word came down that Marsh went rogue. I need privacy if this is going to work."

Bill pushed me into the room and turned the chair so I saw both Jyanette and Kate in the doorway.

"Don't worry," Kate told Jyanette. "I won't screw your boyfriend."

Jyanette has a very dark skin tone, a hereditary trait from her African mother, but I saw the tiniest amount of color in her dark cheeks and knew she was blushing, only because I knew the signs. Anyone else would have missed it.

Little intimate things like that are why I still loved her. Tiny telltale signs I see plainly, while others don't notice them because they're too subtle to be seen by an untrained eye.

Kate shut the door, and I moved to the bed.

"You and the lawyer are getting back together again, huh?" she said quietly.

Now it was my turn to blush, and with my fair skin it was obvious.

"I don't know."

"But it's what you want?"

"Kate, I—"

"It's okay, Len. It's been a fun few months, and the sex was good, but to be honest — you're really not my type. And looking at Ms. Emery just now, I think your odds are good."

"Really?" I said. I couldn't keep the excitement out of my voice.

"Whatever. Now, lie back and let me guide you. What are we looking for? The last canister, right?"

"Yeah, I keep getting distracted by these two glowing orbs."

Kate frowned. "Orbs?"

"Yes. I try to reach out, to know where to go and I keep seeing them. They're blocking me."

"Don't fight it. Maybe these orbs are part of the message."

"Okay," I said and closed my eyes.

Kate began to do the relaxation technique to put me into a light trance, but I was distracted. Was she right? Did something Kate notice suggest I might have a chance to get back with Jyanette? She was a profiler, her job was reading people. My mind raced with ideas of what I would attempt to do after this was all over.

"Len," Kate said in a stern voice. "You're letting your mind wander, and not in the right direction."

"Sorry," I apologized. "I've had a lot of distractions tonight."

"Well, get with it, or I'll phone that German mentor of yours and have him yell at you."

This got a smile from me. I wouldn't put it past her, and I knew she could get Doctor Kohl to do it.

"Now, use your training, I can't do it all by myself."

I closed my eyes and focused on my breath, listening intently as Kate walked me through the relaxation exercise. I allowed myself to go deeper into a trance state.

Kate was speaking in a calm, relaxed tone. "Tell me what you see."

I saw myself surrounded by darkness and fog. In the distance were the two glowing orbs, one bright blue the other a tawny brown.

"I see the orbs," I said, "floating in the distance."

"These orbs have significance to you, allow yourself to understand what they mean. Move toward them."

In the empty place my mind had created, I began to move toward the orbs. This was a different feeling, unlike when I was in the RV with Lindwall and his men. In that case, I was projecting my consciousness into a place. This was a memory, something I had witnessed that was planted into my subconscious, but my conscious mind couldn't quite get it.

I kept moving forward, and the orbs, instead of getting larger as I drew nearer, were shrinking. As they grew smaller, they also seemed more familiar.

As they continued to shrink, black circles appeared in the middle of them and then the pair of them blinked.

The image cleared in my mind.

They were eyes, a pair of mis-matched *eyes*, one blue and one brown, looking down at me just over the edge of a mask.

All at once, I was back in the hospital isolation room and there was the female doctor with the clipboard in her hand.

She spoke but her words seemed to drag, as if she were speaking in slow-motion. "I will be off duty. Doctor Patel will be taking over, if you're okay with foreigners."

I recalled my puzzled reaction at this comment. "What?"

She sighed, and it seemed to take a long time. "He's from India, but seems to know what he's doing, not like some people around here."

Like the blacks...

It was the mental impression I had received from her, and I could sense what was behind those bicolored eyes.

There was an animus towards people of color. No, it was more than that... it was pure hatred.

Hospital...

It was suddenly crystal clear, and so obvious I wanted to kick myself for missing it. If the virus were released, where would the victims be taken? To Mountainside Medical Center, the premier hospital in the area.

What if the virus were released *there*?

There were people with weakened immune systems, who were already fighting for their lives. The virus was sure to be fatal to them. Plus, it could infect the staff and the doctors, all the professionals who might have a chance to stop the disease.

It was diabolical, and so very clever.

Lindwall was many things, a racist, a true hater, and a monster — but he wasn't stupid. He had a member of the Faction at the hospital.

I struggled to try to recall her name while I was in this deep state. Something with an 'M'. It was Masters, Monsters... no... Miller! Her name was Doctor Miller.

"Bring me up," I said, as I worked to pull myself out of the trance state.

Kate used her hypnotic technique to bring me to full consciousness, unlike our previous work, where I jumped up out of the trance.

This technique was much less jarring.

I sat up and looked at her. "The hospital, the final canister is somewhere in the hospital."

"Oh my God," she gasped.

19. DYING TO GET IN

The advantage of being at MPD was that all the communications and several of the team leaders were there in one place.

Kate ran out of the room to get Bill, as I got out of bed and into the wheelchair. I had to go with them, because I could pinpoint the location of the canister faster than the guys using their radar scanner.

At this point I was running on little more than adrenaline, and my leg ached as well as my other scrapes and bruises.

The hallway looked like a schoolyard where the kids had just been released. People all about, hustling and bustling to get ready or get moving.

Word had spread fast.

Bill and Jyanette appeared and Bill pushed my chair back into the outer hall of the bunk rooms. He leaned close. "Len, do you have any idea how a canister could have gotten into the hospital?"

"Yes, through a member of the staff, a Doctor Miller. When I met her, I got strange impressions from her," I told him.

Jyanette was holding a tablet and scrolling. "There is a Doctor Thomasina Miller listed on staff. It says her expertise is infectious diseases."

Tommy…

The name flashed through my mind. "Tommy, that could be a nickname for Thomasina. Bill, I'm *sure* it's her. I heard Lindwall talking about someone named Tommy."

"This is a serious charge, Len," Bill said. "And less to go on than even your usual readings."

"I *know* the canister is at the hospital. Think about it! It's part of the overall plan. If people had been infected at the bus terminal or the train depot, they would have been taken to Mountainside Medical Center. Now, if health care professionals came down with the virus…"

"A panic would ensue," Jyanette added.

Bill glanced to Jyanette and she returned his gaze solemnly. "You're right, Len, we can't risk it. The teams are getting ready to move. You and I will go out ahead and see if we can locate this canister."

"I'm coming with you," Jyanette announced.

"So am I," came another female voice from behind us. Kate stood in the doorway, her arms folded and her jaw set.

Bill shook his head. "I think just Len and me—"

"And what if he runs into a problem?" Kate said. "I can use hypnosis to help him, if he needs it."

"Ladies," I protested. "We just don't want either of you to be in danger."

Jyanette turned to me, fury in her eyes. "You look here, *Doctor.* Your ass would be grass if I hadn't saved it. Consider me your freakin' bodyguard."

Kate smiled at this, and gave Jyanette an admiring glance.

Bill was not pleased. "Very well, but we have to move it, and move it *fast*. I'll get clearance from Captain Harris and Gabe Petrie, so they can call ahead to the hospital and tell them we're coming."

He bolted out of the room before anyone could argue.

Kate and Jyanette exchanged looks, and they seemed to be communicating wordlessly. Both wore small grins as if a funny secret had passed between them. It was disconcerting that two women who had both seen me naked were able to communicate about me and I had no idea what was being exchanged.

I may be a psychic, but how women can convey information with unspoken signals is still a mystery to me.

After only a moment of silence, where I felt like I was intruding on a silent conversation between the two ladies, Bill was back in the doorway. He was wearing a tactical vest emblazoned with 'POLICE' in iridescent letters. He also had a duty belt around his waist with a firearm, extra magazines, and other gear. He carried a second vest which he handed to me.

He looked at the two women. "We're moving out as soon as you two are in vests."

The ladies didn't argue and left the room. I pulled my jacket off over my head and Bill gave me a hand getting into the vest. I didn't have any gear, but I put my wallet and keys into two of the pockets.

"Is this necessary, Bill?"

"You were attacked at the bus depot. What if Lindwall has someone assigned to guard the canister at the hospital? I've also been meaning to give you this—"

He handed me my cell phone. The screen had a crack in it, but when I pushed the button, it lit up and was still functional.

"I found this in the parking lot when I tried to call you."

"Thanks for rescuing it," I said, and slipped it into one of the pockets on the vest.

He pushed me into the hall, where we were met by Jyanette and Kate. While Jyanette's vest read "POLICE," Kate's vest was marked "FBI" and she had a duty belt with a sidearm as well.

"Kate," I said. "I've never seen you with a weapon."

"I'm trained in the use of firearms, and probably could outshoot you on a gun range," Kate said, patting the pistol.

I had no doubt, as I had only held a gun a few times in my life.

We moved to the parking lot with Bill pushing me. Flakes of snow began to fall around us, lightly.

"Great, that's all we need," Bill muttered.

"It's only flurries, Bill," Jyanette said, looking up into the night sky.

We moved as a group to one of the large police SUVs, marked with the identification of the Mountainview Police.

"Not taking the unmarked?" I asked.

"This has more room, plus we'll need sirens and lights, and to be able to park it anywhere we need to," Bill explained. Jyanette helped me out of the chair and into the back seat, and she got into the front passenger seat. Kate joined me in back as Bill folded the wheelchair and put it in the hatchback, I held my cane between my legs.

We were off, sirens blaring and lights flashing. In moments, we headed for the nearby hospital. The snow picked up in intensity, but was still only a light amount.

It was almost midnight by this time, and I was hoping that the timer on the final canister would be set for hours later. If Tommy, aka Doctor Miller, had heard on the news about the other canisters, I hoped that she didn't set it for an earlier release.

We travelled through the dark streets, all of us focused on our mission. I watched the falling snowflakes, unsure if they were a blessing or a curse. Moving those huge mobile labs through snow was not the best situation.

Bill broke the silence in the car. "Len, I'm thinking the first place to look would be the heating system."

"That makes sense," Jyanette agreed.

"I don't think so. That hospital uses hydronic heating," Kate explained. "With all the different rooms and air circulation limitations, that's how they can heat the buildings safely. I think Mountainside uses steam for heat."

"Steam heat?" I questioned. "Isn't that kind of old-fashioned?"

"No," Kate assured me. "The steam is also used for sterilization and humidification. It also means that any virus that gets into the heating tower wouldn't spread through the air ducts. We should be glad it's winter, because in summer the AC would be going and that has to use the ducts."

"Good to know," Jyanette said. "What other places should we consider?"

Kate pondered this. "Somewhere on the main floors, so the virus could spread upward."

Bill piped up. "The elevators would be a good idea."

"Hard to manage," Jyanette replied. "The only place to put it would be on the top of the car, and there are cameras in the elevator. Security would see you setting up the tank."

"So it would have to be someplace where there aren't cameras," I theorized.

"That puts the heating tower out of the picture then," Kate said. "There are numerous cameras there, and I'm sure security would act if anyone, even a doctor, went into it unauthorized."

Suddenly it hit me. "The ladies' room."

Bill was watching the road, but the two women looked at me.

"Of course," Jyanette said, making the same realization as I had.

"I get it," Kate agreed. "You take an overnight shift and slip the tank into the facility and place it in the ladies' room."

Jyanette was looking at Kate and nodding. "Nurses would get exposed, and every time the door opened the atomized virus could travel into the hall."

McGee remarked. "I hate to bring this up, but a hospital that size has *dozens* of bathrooms."

"It will be a public one, multiple stalls," I said, the idea becoming clear in my mind. "It would have to be near the ICU."

"Why?" Jyanette asked.

Kate snapped her fingers. "Simple! If the nurses and doctors treating sick people became sick as well, then the rumor would start that the virus could get through personal protective equipment."

I nodded. "While the truth was, they caught the virus outside of the ICU or isolation rooms because of a visit to the ladies' room."

"That would add to the panic," Jyanette speculated.

"People would leave town out of fear, some of them already exposed," Bill said. "I have to admit, if Lindwall and his cohorts were after a public hysteria, this would be a good way to start one."

We arrived at the Mountainside Medical Center and Bill pulled the car to the curb.

Two men in long coats with patches on the shoulders were standing outside in the snow as we drove up. One moved towards the SUV as it stopped. He stepped up to the driver's side window and asked, "Lieutenant McGee?"

Bill nodded and opened the door, and the man met him with a firm handshake with his gloved hand. "I'm Captain Grant, head of security for the hospital."

The man was almost the same size as McGee, though he had a larger gut and white hair.

The snow was falling more heavily now and there was a hush over the area. Cars were few and far between, and the snow dampened the sounds of highways and trains.

I thought of the previous December, when I was forced to face the follower of a murderous cult. It had snowed that night as well. For me, snow was becoming an ominous portent.

Jyanette had retrieved my wheelchair and our little group went up the snowy sidewalk and into the hospital.

"Captain Grant," I heard McGee say. "We're an advance group and we have some ideas as to where we need to look."

Grant spoke in low tones. "Lieutenant, your captain was pretty vague. He said some feds would be coming. Is this some kind of terrorist attack or something?"

"Yes, Captain, using compressed air tanks," McGee explained. "I'll do my best to keep you in the loop, but we may need to evacuate part or all of the hospital. The last thing I want is a panic."

"Agreed," Grant responded. "Compressed air tanks? We have hundreds of those between oxygen and liquid gases. Do you have some kind of detection equipment?"

McGee nodded. "You could say that. In the meantime, I need one of your men with me to stay in radio contact with you."

Grant indicated the other man, a tall African-American gentleman. "Jim's my LT. There's no one I trust more."

The man was only six feet tall but looked smaller due to the proximity of the hulking Grant and McGee. He nodded to McGee, and our group started moving, Grant heading for the large security desk. It was in the middle of the open lobby foyer and was elevated on a circular dais to give it some height. Three short steps led up to the desk from all sides of the circle.

Kate spoke to the security lieutenant. "We need to go to the ICU wing."

"That's not a problem, ma'am," Jim answered.

He led us to the elevator and as the door closed, I looked out through the front glass wall to see the snow descending, fear clutched at my stomach. I reached back to Jyanette. Her hand was like ice. She let go of the wheelchair grip and took my hand in hers. We soon reached the third floor and the doors opened.

"The only thing I ask is that we be as quiet as possible," Jim asserted.

We all nodded silently in reply as we moved into the wide hall.

"Is there a public rest room on this floor?" McGee asked.

"Several," Jim replied as we walked slowly and quietly. "Mostly a lot of individual ones…"

Jyanette, who had let my hand go to continue to push me, spoke up. "We're looking for one with multiple stalls."

Jim gestured up ahead. "That would be right here."

A few feet down the hall were a pair of bathrooms, one marked "Men" and one "Ladies."

Outside the window, multicolored lights flashed and McGee looked out.

"SWAT team is here," he said and pulled out his phone to consult with the commander.

"Jyanette, let's make sure the bathroom's empty," Kate suggested.

"On it," Jyanette said, and the pair of them headed through the door.

Jim watched the retreating Jyanette with a look I was all too familiar with. I almost wanted to say, "Hands off, she's mine," but she wasn't, even if I wanted her to be.

I couldn't blame the guy for looking.

She was magnificent.

The pair returned and gave the all-clear, and I wheeled into the tiled room. I looked at the drop ceiling tiles knowing that's where I would hide something. I closed my eyes and pictured the mismatched eyes of Doctor Miller.

I opened my eyes, but I had pushed myself into an altered state. The room around me had been drained of color and everything in my line of vision was dull, black and white tones, void of depth and flat looking. I knew I was having a vision, which was reinforced when Doctor Thomasina Miller shoved open the door and passed right through the very real body of Jyanette. She entered pushing a wheelchair that was as much a phantom as she was.

On the seat of the chair was a gas canister. It was smaller than the others I had seen. Though I only saw sepia tones I could see that it was more than one color, and had a decal wrapped around it with 'OXYGEN' in capital letters.

I stared at this container that only I could see, and immediately recognized where I had seen it previously. When I had walked into the RV, I glimpsed a memory from Lanie, as she looked up and saw Godfrey with the gas mask and gloves, right before he sprayed her in the face with the cold, atomized mist. The canister he'd been holding had the same markings, disguising it to look like a tank of oxygen.

This was why Doctor Miller so easily brought the canister into the hospital — no one would question a doctor with an oxygen tank! Even when she was pushing it in a wheelchair, people would assume it was for a patient.

The tank was crowned with a 'gizmo' on the top. The device was a small rectangular box, with a gray and black digital readout, and a small nozzle at the highest point. It must be the atomizer with the built-in timer. There was also a small black plastic extension about the size of a drinking straw, which I realized with trepidation was an antenna. It sat on top of the atomizer with a flashing red LED next to it.

The shadowy image passed through Jyanette a second time and into the first stall. Doctor Miller proceeded to stand on top of the ring of the commode and push up the ceiling tile in the corner. She glanced around at the supports and the grid work that held the drop ceiling in place.

She carefully removed the tile and I could see up into the opening. There was a ledge on top of the wall that was blocked by the ceiling tile, and a metal bracket with a strap hanging from it.

She opened the strap and stepped down off the commode to retrieve the canister. I was focused on watching her, but I noticed that both Kate and Jyanette were looking at me and their mouths were moving.

I closed my eyes and let the vision go.

"—feeling okay?" Kate was saying.

"Yeah, sorry, I had a vision," I said, taking deep breaths to ground myself. "This is it, this is where she put the tank. There's some kind of holder hidden in the wall, above the ceiling."

I pointed at the overhead tile above the first stall, and Jyanette moved towards it.

Danger...

"Jyanette, don't!" I barked, making her jump. "There's something wrong, another booby trap or something. I think opening the ceiling will set it off."

"We should move out and let the hazmat guys seal off this room," Jyanette said.

"I don't know if it will help. If the virus is leaked into the space between the drop ceiling and the real one, it could infect this entire floor."

"We need to evacuate this part of the hospital," Kate said.

Without another word, Jyanette pushed me out of the door with Kate right behind us.

"This is the place," Jyanette said to McGee.

"Did you see the tank?" McGee worried.

"It's in the drop ceiling above the first stall," I told Bill. "I'm sensing danger. It's either not safe or boobytrapped, and I'm not sure which. Even worse, it has an antenna."

"An antenna?" Bill repeated. "That can't be good."

Jim, the security lieutenant, stepped over to us. "You said you're sensing danger? What does that mean?"

"It means that no one else goes into that room without a hazmat suit," Bill stated firmly. "And we have to move anyone and everyone we can out of the immediate area."

Jim was frowning. "Because this guy says he *senses* danger?"

"No," McGee responded. "Because *I* say we need to move back and move people out. Contact your captain."

Persuaded or not, Jim grabbed his radio and began to talk to Captain Grant.

I looked down the hall and saw we were not that far from the nurses station and the isolation wards. I realized that when I made my escape earlier, I had been outside the ladies' room when I got the buzz of 'danger.'

I had gone a long way only to return to the same place, but now the danger was close and very immediate.

20. UNFILTERED TRANSMISSION

Bill remained with Jim to guard the ladies' room, while Jyanette, Kate, and I returned to the security desk. From the main desk looking out through the glass wall, we saw the portable laboratory drive up a few short minutes later.

The huge vehicle had a hard time negotiating the hill, as the snow was getting deeper. There were at least two inches on the ground as the snow fell in huge heavy flakes, and the conditions were becoming treacherous.

The security men were kind enough to move us into their break room, which was a canteen with a table and several chairs. I tried to go into a trance again and find out what the exact nature of the booby trap could be, but I had no luck.

Like drugs and alcohol, exhaustion and lack of sleep can muddle my abilities, and I couldn't seem to put myself into a trance. I was afraid that if I closed my eyes, I would just fall asleep.

We were in a corner in the break room and Kate and Jyanette were peppering me with questions.

"So, if it's booby-trapped, how?" Kate demanded.

"I don't know—"

"You said there was a holder for the tank," Jyanette argued. "Was it there before or did she put it there?"

"I'm not sure—"

"Is the team in danger even in their hazmat suits?" Kate added.

I held up my hands to stop them both. "Look, I saw what I saw, and didn't get much further than what I told you already. I don't even know if I can tap into that vision now that I'm out of the room where it occurred."

"But you got one of those buzzes of yours?" Jyanette said.

"I know, but there's something I'm missing," I protested.

"What?" Kate asked.

"Something about the tank she planted," I explained.

"You told us it was disguised as an oxygen tank," Kate urged. "Was there something else?"

"Yes, it was… smaller."

Jyanette and Kate exchanged a glance.

"Maybe it just looked smaller?" Jyanette wondered. "You said it had a paint job and a label?"

"Maybe," I said, rubbing my neck. I wanted to lie down and sleep for a month. "What if the assessment of the number of tanks is incorrect?"

Kate frowned at this. "What do you mean?"

I pulled out my phone, hit the number for Bill, and put the call on speaker so all three of us could hear.

"McGee," came his gruff voice.

"Bill, the information you told me when I was in isolation, that four tanks had been delivered to the guy who created the virus at his lab. Did you see the actual invoice?"

"No, I was told ... well, the *team* was told at one of the meetings."

"By whom?"

Bill hesitated for a moment. "I think it was Marsh."

"Marsh?" I repeated. "You mean, the guy who was working with Lindwall?"

"Do you think the information is suspect?"

"Bill, I've got a strange feeling that there are *five* tanks."

"Five tanks?"

"Yes, they either had that many originally or perhaps there was a way to transfer the contents of one tank into two, I don't know."

Bill considered this. "Did you say that the one in your vision in the ladies room had an antenna?"

"That's right."

"It might be on a radio circuit of some kind."

"What would that do?"

"Back when I was FBI, a trick terrorists would use was to have a bomb on a radio frequency so that if you defused or detonated it, the loss of the radio signal would trigger another bomb nearby. It's not a technique known to the general public."

I looked up at the women, who were both aghast. Bill was silent on the other end of the phone.

"Bill, don't touch that tank until I try to find out if there's another one," I insisted.

"Homeland Security is already sealing off the ICU hallway with a plastic tent, going up into the ceiling."

"Give me a few minutes," I said. "Do you know where Captain Grant might be?"

"He's here with me now. You want to speak to him?"

"Please put him on."

The gruff voice came over my phone. "Who's this?"

"It's Doctor Wise, the guy in the wheelchair."

"Oh, yeah. What do you need, Doc?"

"Who was on desk duty last night?"

"On the overnight, that would be Willis. He's on now, manning the desk, while we try to handle this mess."

"I'd like to talk to him, with your permission, Captain."

"I'll radio him to cooperate in any way that he can."

"Thanks," I said ending the call, and wheeling toward the door.

"We're coming with you," Kate said, as Jyanette grabbed the push handles and began to move me forward.

I sat back and allowed them to wheel me near the security desk. The lobby was now filled with helmeted men with large guns and black attire, the letters on their vests reading "FBI," "DHS," and "POLICE." They made very little noise for such a large contingency, as they waited to move into action when needed.

We reached the security desk, and behind it was a young man in his twenties. He had short brown hair and a physique that suggested a great deal of work with weights. He was watching the federal agents with a longing that suggested he was desirous to join their ranks. A lot of people who end up in security work are former cops and military, and the young ones are those who long to be.

He looked over as we approached. He glanced at us, then around the room again, as if taking in everything. He returned his attention to us with a tight smile as I got close enough to speak.

"Are you Mister Willis?"

"Yes, sir," he responded, with a glance up to the two ladies as well.

"I understand you were on duty last night?" I said.

"That is correct, sir," Willis replied.

"Did you see Doctor Miller any time during the night?"

"Yes," the man told me and smiled. "She came in pushing an oxygen tank in a wheelchair. It wasn't normal protocol, but she said we were running low, and another hospital gave us a tank to tide us over."

Jyanette spoke up. "This is very important. Could there have been *two* oxygen tanks?"

"I only saw one, ma'am," Willis said.

Lying...

The buzz struck me very strongly and I paused to look hard at the young man. Why would he lie about something like that?

I focused on him until he made eye contact with me. "Are you sure?"

And there was the image in his mind: Doctor Miller, who he thought was hot, pushing the wheelchair. And on the seat were a pair of tanks marked "OXYGEN." Both had the timer on top, and worse, both had an antenna.

"Yes, sir I am."

Lying...

"Thank you, you've been very helpful," I said, and pulled away from Jyanette toward the elevator.

One of the black-suited men moved forward, and I realized it was Gabe Petrie. I'd never seen the man in full tactical gear before and it gave me pause.

"Where are you going?" Gabe said. "We can't let you up there."

"Agent Petrie," I said, using his official title for once. "I need to get upstairs to the tank we located. I think I can use it to help me locate a second one."

"Len," Kate stressed in a quiet voice. "You just heard what the man on duty said. There was only one tank."

I kept my voice low. "He's lying."

"Look, Doc," Petrie complained. "We're not allowing anyone up there until the hazmat team has sealed the area and disarmed the device. Besides, if there is another canister, where is it?"

"I don't know, yet. I'm hoping I can get an idea from the other tank, if I get near it."

Petrie looked over at all the men. "Tell you what, we'll start scanning with radar—"

Danger...

"No, don't," I said as the buzz hit me. "The tank we found upstairs had an antenna and could be sensitive to any kind of radio waves."

"How would they know we'd be using radar?"

"Agent Marsh, that's how," Jyanette said. "What if Marsh told Lindwall you would be using radar to look through walls?"

I broke in. "The point is, McGee said if there were two canisters they might be on a circuit. I think the radar might interfere with that and set it off."

Petrie shook his head. "I suppose you have a better idea?"

"If I can get a reading on the first tank, I might be able to track where the other one is hidden."

"Doc, be reasonable. I can't allow you to go up there."

I wanted to shake the man, but before I could Kate moved between us. "Len, I can regress you, bring you to the vision you had. We can do that right in the security break room."

Jyanette frowned. "You think it will work?"

"Let's try it," I said with a sigh. "Gabe, can you just give me a few minutes before anyone tries to disarm that tank we found?"

"They're still sealing the hallway," Gabe said with a look to his watch. "You have a half-hour."

"Thanks," I said, as Jyanette turned me around and headed us back to the security break room.

I phoned Bill again.

"Yeah, now what?"

"The security guard, Willis, saw Doctor Miller with two tanks last night. She gave him some cock-and-bull story that they borrowed oxygen from another hospital."

"What do you need me to do?"

"Gabe Petrie gave us a half-hour while the hazmat team seals the hallway. Make sure he gives it to us. I am going to try to locate the final canister."

"On it, Len. Let me know what you find."

I ended the call, and Jyanette wheeled me to a corner next to a chair where Kate could sit.

Jyanette spoke up. "Len, do you really think that security guard was lying?"

"I do."

"Then I'm going to go keep an eye on him as well," she said and moved to the door.

"Alone at last," Kate joked.

"Come on, we're on the clock," I snapped.

"Where do you want to go?"

"I got an image of two tanks in the wheelchair from the security guy, Willis. Let me use that as a focal point, but I'm having a lot of trouble getting into a trance."

"I'll help you," Kate said, and she began to talk me down into a hypnotic state. It was a fight, because my brain wanted to fall asleep but the aches and pains from this night were helping to keep me awake.

She did simple relaxation techniques, and I recalled the image of the wheelchair pushed by Doctor Miller as seen by the guard, Willis. I focused on her, and even more on her bicolored eyes.

Then, all at once, I was in the lobby. The huge open space now had the sepia tones of a memory. I was watching from Willis' point of view as Miller approached pushing the wheelchair. I followed his eyes as they peeked at his watch to note that it was two-thirty AM. Outside the glass wall, the sky was dark and even the outdoor lighting was subdued by this time of night.

He looked at Miller as she drew near, her mouth was moving, but I heard no words. Sometimes I get visions that are in full color and sound, as when I visited Lindwall in his trailer. This was not one of those times, and although Miller was speaking, I heard nothing.

She rolled right up to the security desk, her lips still moving. Then the point of view I was looking through, Willis', got up from the desk, and went to the wheelchair to pick up one of the canisters resting on it.

It was the absolute duplicate of the one I had seen in the previous vision, complete with the digital readout, and even the antenna. The image froze in my mind.

I spoke out loud. "Willis."

"What?" I heard Kate ask from what sounded like a hundred miles away.

"Willis took one of the canisters from Miller," I said.

"Stay with it Leonard," Kate's voice told me. "See where he puts it."

I took a deep breath and returned to the scene, the image of Willis taking the tank. As Miller waved to him and continued on her way, I saw him move back to the desk.

He put the tank on the floor, and the point of view changed as he looked *under* the desk. There was a small rectangular panel built in the floor, and I saw his hand pull out a knife and pry this panel open very carefully.

Removing the panel revealed an empty space and his hands picked up the tank, and carefully fit it in. It fit perfectly and I realized that the reason for the smaller tank was because it had been intended to be hidden there the entire time.

The hands grabbed the rectangle of flooring and slipped it back into place.

That's when the realization hit me. What place would there be no cameras, besides the bathrooms?

The security desk itself.

"Bring me up," I muttered to Kate. "As fast as you can."

She began a backward count, giving calm commands to guide me up out of the trance. As I was brought up to full consciousness, I had an adrenalin rush that almost made me fly out of the wheelchair.

"The security desk," I gasped. "The canister is under the security desk."

"Holy shit!" Kate barked. "What do we do?"

I yanked out my phone. "You go tell Gabe he needs to evacuate that lobby. And don't let Willis get away."

Kate headed for the door as I hit the number for Jyanette on my phone.

"Yes, Len."

"Willis, the guard, is he at the desk?"

"No, he just got up and told one of the other guards that he had to do a round of the exterior buildings."

Danger…

My buzzes that night had all been coming to me too late to help in any of the situations I found myself.

"The final canister is under the security desk, and I have a feeling that it will soon be set off."

"Oh God!"

"Jyanette, get out of there, get outside," I yelled into the phone as I wheeled into the hall and headed for the desk.

As I rolled I yelled out as soon as I saw someone. "Evacuate! There's a canister in the lobby. *Get everyone out!*"

Gabe Petrie raced to the door and yelled for everyone to get out. My guess was that Kate had seen Willis was gone and come to the same conclusion I did. If he was part of the Faction, he knew that the hidden tank would soon start to release its contents and had left while he still had time.

At best, we had minutes before the lobby and the ICU were contaminated by the virus. Anyone caught here without a protective suit was as good as dead.

---

21. BLIGHT UPON THEE

O utside, people rushed around in the eerie silence of the snow-filled night. By now it was snowing with heavy flakes and visibility was low, creating a sense of the surreal in the dim glow of the street lamps.

Two people in full protective suits, looking like spacemen, stood near Gabe Petrie. One was a man, the other a woman, and they wore white suits that covered their entire body, complete with a plexiglass front on their helmets and a separate air supply on an impressive belt unit.

I was too far away to hear what they were saying, but I saw Petrie get an annoyed look on his face and point over at me.

To save anyone trouble I tried to wheel my way over to them, but the snow made my chair slip and slide a bit. I was surprised when Jyanette grabbed the back and steadied me. She pushed me forward, sliding the chair through the snow like a sled.

"Where is this canister, Wise?" Petrie demanded as he moved toward me.

"Under the security desk, there's a panel in the floor that can be pried up," I explained.

"Who is this?" the woman said through the tinny speaker of her PPE garment. Through the plexiglass helmet, I could see that she was of Asian descent and only about five-foot-four.

Petrie did not seem pleased. "Doctor Leonard Wise, he's a consultant for the Mountainview PD." He glared at the two and added. "You heard him! Get in there."

Danger…

I felt the buzz, and it was followed by another.

Must go with them…

There are times I wished I didn't get my insights. This was one of them.

I was outside, safe and sound, and Jyanette and Kate were both nearby. I was sure McGee would be evacuated shortly. Here I was, getting the mental impression I had to go back in with them, putting myself in danger. That was Jyanette's biggest complaint, and I wanted desperately to show her I was more responsible than in the past. Yet here I was feeling an overwhelming need to go back in with the team of professionals.

I held up my hands. "Wait, don't go in. I need to go with you."

"*What?*" Gabe Petrie exploded.

"*What?*" Jyanette yelped at almost the same moment.

The two scientists or technicians exchanged looks, and then turned to me.

"Come *with* us?" the man questioned, his voice distorted by the speaker. "Just what kind of a doctor are you?"

Admitting I was a parapsychologist would not inspire confidence.

"Look, the canister in there has some kind of booby trap and I think I can help you to not set it off. I won't touch anything, I'll just observe."

Petrie's jaw was set, and his appearance suggested he had just sucked on a lemon. I *had* located the other canisters, and if there was a chance to avoid a biological catastrophe, he was willing to take it.

"You got an extra suit?" Petrie asked the pair.

The male half of the space-suit team gazed back at the large mobile lab and spoke through his speaker. "Yes, an extra one in the lab, but I don't know if we can push the chair through the snow—"

I interrupted. "How about I put it on right there under that overhang?" I pointed to a spot near the door where there was no snow. "I can do it quickly, and leave the chair at the door, if you'll help me."

The man nodded and strode purposefully toward the lab.

Jyanette leaned next to my ear, concern evident in her voice. "Why are you doing this?"

"I have to," I insisted. "There's something in there that they won't be expecting, and my presence might make all the difference." I turned to look up at her. "But please stay out here. If it goes wrong, I'll be okay, but only if I know you're safe."

She sighed and shook her head. "Just don't get more damaged than you currently are."

"I'll do my best," I said as I gazed into her brown eyes. Yes, I wanted to come back in one piece, if for no other reason than to have a chance to look into those eyes.

She slid the chair back to the overhang. Once out of the snow, the wheels turned again. The woman in the PPE suit joined us.

"By the way, I'm Len," I told the woman, and she met my eyes.

"I'm Julie," she said. "You're a consultant? Are you an expert in these kind of devices or something? What do you do?"

Risk my life most times.

"I'm more of a profiler than anything else," I offered. I thought that sounded vague enough.

Her male counterpart arrived, half-carrying, half-dragging the heavy PPE suit.

I used my cane to get upright. Both of the technicians as well as Jyanette helped me put on the suit. I had to take off my winter coat, my sports coat, the tactical vest, and even my shoes which made me feel the cold all the more.

I got into the suit one leg at a time and then pulled it up to my neck and zipped it closed. Then I returned to the chair to put on the tall rubber boots that went up past my ankles, and sealed the leg cuffs. I stood again, as the heavy belt with the air supply was wrapped around my waist and the man instructed Jyanette how to attach the hose.

I then put on the helmet and Jyanette helped with the seal, as I put on not one, but three pairs of gloves, the final pair sealing the sleeves.

Jyanette looked at me and moved her mouth, but I couldn't hear her. Julie, the female scientist, pointed at the belt and she hit a switch which activated the built-in sound system.

"Can you hear me, Len?" Jyanette said.

"Quite well," I replied, though I was sure my own voice was distorted a bit.

"You're sealed in, Doctor Wise," the man said, checking another device on the overlarge belt pack.

"Thanks. I'm Len, and I met Julie. What's your name?"

"Harry. The lobby's been evacuated and the team is setting up an isolation tent, but we should get inside out of the cold."

Jyanette remained outside as we shuffled back into the building. Harry had been correct, and I saw men and women inside wearing PPE equipment, though not as constrictive as ours. They had set up a rectangular tent made of a frame of white plastic poles, that I realized were PVC plumbing pipes. Over it, heavy clear plastic wrapped three of the four sides, and were held on the floor by chains sewn into the bottom hem. As we watched, two people placed the final curtain into position, which was the top of the rectangle as well as the final side. Two other people used clear duct tape to seal the plastic once it was correctly situated. The amazing thing was that they had built this tent in the few minutes since we'd alerted them about the canister's location.

"Wow!" I exclaimed. "What is that?"

Harry turned to look at me. In the space suit, he had to turn his entire body. "It's an Airborne Isolation Tent. Since it's all made with PVC pipes, we can cut and glue the parts together very quickly."

I nodded. "You make the design you need in the space you have?"

"Yes," Julie responded. "They've been building one upstairs and they opened up the drop ceiling to totally seal off the ladies' bathroom."

"Do you know how they found these tanks without using the scanning system?" Harry asked as we drew near the tent.

I felt it best not to say that I was the one who had told the team the locations. I was feeling a bit unsure of myself at this point, as no one else had seen the canisters except me, and then only in a vision.

My recent failure at the house the team had raided ran through my mind.

Instead, I changed the subject. "How do we get in the tent?"

"There are two cuts in the front with zippers like a plastic bag," Harry explained.

"Once we're in, it's totally sealed," Julie added.

We waited as the six people who had set it up evacuated the room, leaving us next to the transparent tent. Even with my cane as a help, my leg was in a great deal of pain, and I found it hard to walk due to the extra weight of the equipment belt. I was shuffling along rather than walking.

"I'll go first," Julie offered, and pulled the loose flap aside to step in.

"Let me hold it for you, Len," Harry said and held up the flap as I made my way in slowly.

Harry came in last, and then ran a pair of plastic tabs downward that sealed the lip on the doors.

"There's a panel under the desk," I said and pointed. The chair had been removed when the tent was being put into place.

Harry pulled a tool from his belt resembling a screwdriver combined with a putty knife. It had a flat edge, as well as a curve on the blade that I am sure contained a knife edge.

Julie had a flashlight on a wrist strap around her right arm. She shone the light into the kneehole under the desk.

"I see it," Harry said and moved into place.

I leaned against the desk for support. It was a big desk solidly connected to the floor, with numerous displays showing camera views of different parts of the building. Each one clicked to a different location every ten seconds or so. It was unnerving that this ever-changing video display was going on while our focus was on the flooring.

Harry was about to insert the tool in the left corner, when I got a buzz.

Wrong side…

"Wait," I said. "Open it from the other side."

Harry looked up at me, annoyed. "What difference does it make?"

"I'm not sure, but trust me."

"Do what he says, Harry," Julie urged. "Let's get on with this."

Harry shrugged. He moved the tool to the other side and began to pry.

"And don't open it all the way," I advised. "Let's see how it's set up in there. The other canisters were all booby-trapped."

"All right, all right," Harry seethed.

The tool seemed to gain purchase, and he slowly raised up the panel.

Danger…

"Easy," I encouraged. "Go easy."

As he leaned the panel slowly up, the light revealed the canister hidden down in the underfloor space. We also saw a pair of wires connected to the display on the top of the tank going to the side of the panel that Harry had originally wanted to open.

Harry froze, not opening it anymore. "Geez, what are those wires for?"

Julie moved the light under the lifted panel and into the crack between the panel and the flooring. There was a pair of sensors connected to each wire. One sensor was on the panel and one under the floor.

She spoke up, "I think it's a magnetic switch, like an alarm. Once the circuit is broken, it goes off."

I went down on my one good knee to peer in the open space filled by the tank. This hurt, but not as much as standing. "Julie, put the light on the display."

She moved so the light shone on the liquid crystal display. It read: 30:02, and as I watched it continued counting and was soon below 30. This meant we had only about twenty-nine minutes before the virus was released.

"Julie, hold the panel in place," Harry instructed. "I'll disconnect the magnet from the panel."

As I watched, Julie took hold of the panel and Harry flipped the tool around. In the handle was a hexagonal opening, and Harry plugged a small screwdriver head into it adeptly. He then used it to carefully loosen two tiny screws that held one of the sensors in place.

"Don't let the screws drop," I warned. I wasn't getting any extrasensory insight, but I decided it was a good course of action.

He finished removing the screws and carefully put the two magnets together, to keep the circuit closed. He nodded to Julie and she cautiously lifted the panel and set it on the floor nearby, as Harry did with the screws.

Harry then hit a button on his belt, and spoke into the radio in the suit. "Command, we have a tank with an atomizer and a display that is counting down from 28 minutes at this point. Please advise."

The LCD display was still counting down, as the three of us stared at it.

Freeze...

I felt a shiver run down my spine. I was cold even in this enclosed suit and indoors.

I heard a voice over the speaker in the suit. "This is command. We will have to evac you and hope that the tent can enclose the virus."

Harry spoke up. "Roger that."

Julie turned to him. "Harry, this tent might not hold the spray back. And if it does, for how long? We don't know how intense the pressure in the tank is, or how long it is going to run."

"Julie, I'm a medical technician, not a bomb disposal guy. I have no idea how to stop this thing from going off."

Freeze...

There was that buzz again and I thought it was time I stopped ignoring it.

"Can we freeze it?" I offered.

"What?" Harry said. "It's a tank of liquid nitrogen. How will freezing it help?"

I recalled what I had overheard the first time I saw Lindwall in the RV. He had spoken of the need for a timer that released the liquid nitrogen in slow bursts because to release it all at once would clog the atomizer.

"Lindwall needed an atomizer on a timer," I told him. "If the liquid nitrogen is released all at once, it would freeze the apparatus and stop it from working."

Julie grabbed Harry's arm. "Harry, this makes sense. Back in World War II, the British disarmed German bombs by using liquid nitrogen."

Harry's eyes lit up. "We have two tanks of LN in the lab."

"Get both of them," I said.

Harry turned back to me. "Why?"

"Because if the timers are connected on a radio circuit, we have to freeze both of them at the same time."

"Got it," Harry said, and hit the button on his waist to contact the commander. He switched to a private channel and began to work out the plan to use the liquid nitrogen and to provide a sprayer. He went back and forth as they figured out how to get it together.

"Do you think this will work?" I asked Julie.

Julie looked thoughtful. "My only concern is that they stopped using LN in the last few decades because terrorists started to use temperature sensitive triggers."

I glanced at the timer which continued to countdown. "Since its designed to release liquid nitrogen in slow bursts, I doubt they added a thermal device as well."

Harry turned to us. "We only have one LN sprayer."

I nodded. "Use that on the canister in the ceiling for the ladies room."

"What about here?" Harry asked.

"It's a hole in the floor," Julie explained catching my idea. "We can just pour the LN on top of it. We're in protective suits and we have our own oxygen supply."

"Right, right," Harry said with a peek at the timer.

We had fifteen minutes left at this point.

People in PPE suits were coming into the building. One held a small tank with a nozzle and headed for the elevator, and one wheeled in a large tank on a dolly.

"I'm going to open the channel so we all can hear each other," Harry said and I heard him on the radio in my suit.

"Roger that," came the voice of the commander. "We'll let you know when we're in place."

The tank on the dolly was brought to the outside of our tent with a pair of heavy gloves on top. Julie and Harry quickly opened the flap and wheeled it in, as I moved to the side and sat out of the way on the stone steps. They pulled it off the cart and laid it on the floor with the top directly over the canister. Julie pulled the heavy gloves over her already gloved hands in preparation.

"LN tank and sprayer are in place upstairs," came a voice over the radio in my suit.

"Count it down, please," Harry said.

The main voice started a backward count from ten and as he passed five, Julie pulled the top of the tank loose, and as the voice said, "One," she pulled the top free.

The liquid poured over the tank, flooding the small space. Billows of cold fog sprayed up all around as the super cold liquid hit the warm floor and boiled, changing back from liquid to gas.

From my medical background, I knew that the oxygen levels in this confined space were rapidly becoming far too little for us to breathe. However, since the three of us had our own oxygen supply, we would be unaffected.

The mist was rapidly dissipating, as the room grew colder from the liquefied gas. I pulled myself up to look at the display.

It was dark, all of the electronics completely frozen.

Since Julie had the cryogenic gloves on, she pulled the tank to an upright position. Harry took the multitool and began to take apart the timer and sprayer on top, using a knife in the tool to cut all wires as he went.

I was not getting any buzzes or warning, or anything other than my own pain and weariness.

"Harry," I said. "Permission to leave and get out of this thing."

"Head out to the decontamination tent," Harry said. "Touch only the door, I'll get someone to guide you."

I unzipped one side of the makeshift door and stepped out, as Julie closed it behind me and waved. I saw her lips move in a "thank you," but didn't really hear her.

Cane in hand, taking steps that would have looked more appropriate on an eighty-year-old, I moved to the door, where another man in simple one-piece white coveralls with a gas mask and goggles led me into another tent that had been set up outside.

They had built this decontamination tent on the snow-covered roadway. In the time since I had been inside, large heaters had melted the snow within the tent.

Once I was within, a group of men and women in protective gear hit my suit with water from hoses and scrubbed me with brushes filled with disinfectants.

At the end of the tent, they helped me out of the suit and let me sit on a makeshift bench as I took the oppressive covering off.

"How are you feeling?" a man in a white lab coat asked as he pointed a handheld thermometer at my head.

"I've been better," I groaned.

He looked at the reading and pointed the thermometer at me again. "You have a temperature."

"What?" I said.

"We have to get you into isolation at once."

I could see Jyanette standing near Kate as they got a gurney with a large plastic bag around it. I lay down on it, every part of my body aching, as two men in PPE suits zipped it closed and whisked me back into the hospital in the direction of the isolation ward.

22. PESTILENCE

I slept for twelve hours.

It might have been the painkillers or the exhaustion, or maybe I was truly sick, as I was running a slight fever according to the machines taking all my vitals.

I woke up hungry and signaled the nurse. It was the same woman who had assisted me the previous time, in her paper smock, mask, and gloves.

She scowled at me as she approached the bed. "You're not planning to pull a stunt like last time and sneak out, are you?"

"No," I muttered, feeling slightly ashamed. "I'm happy to stay right here."

"This time, I'm locking the door!"

"In my defense, it was an emergency."

"Well, who knows who you came in contact with?"

I thought of Jyanette and felt worse. What if I had been infected by Lindwall's virus? Would she be infected now?

"Could I please get something to eat?" I attempted to sound contrite.

"All right. We drew blood last night so the doctor will have some test results soon."

"Thank you," I said as she left the room, locking the door as she went.

As I lay there waiting, I thought about Jyanette. Since she broke up with Agent Calvin, would that help my cause? On the other hand—

The phone interrupted my reverie and I looked over to see Bill McGee sitting behind the glass of the outside room.

"Hey, Bill," I said as I picked up the handset.

"How's the hero?" he asked.

"I'd like to be downgraded to plucky sidekick, if that's okay with you."

McGee chuckled. "We got both canisters removed. The liquid nitrogen took out the electronics, and the hazmat team got them sealed and out. They even fixed the ceiling and removed those isolation tents they set up. Come this morning, you couldn't tell they were even here."

"What about the snow?"

"It ended right after they took you away."

"And we have Lindwall locked up?"

"As tight as a caterpillar in a cocoon. We also got Doctor Miller and the security guy, Willis. The pair of them were trying to get out of state but the Pennsylvania State Troopers got them before they even reached East Stroudsburg."

"That's good," I said. "How's Tice?"

Bill's expression grew clouded. "They are treating him with a drug called Dengvaxia which has shown to help people who are infected with the Dengue Virus. From what I understand, they're combining it with isoniazid and rifamycin to work on the

Tuberculous bacteria. It's touch and go, for both him and the Lanie woman."

I was familiar with the antibiotics from my medical training, though the Dengvaxia was new to me. "Did they infect anyone else?"

"So far it doesn't appear they did. We may have contained this, Len."

I nodded and wondered what else I could say. Although Tice had always been a thorn in my craw, I respected him as a cop and a detective. I hated to think he wouldn't be back.

"How are *you* feeling, Len?" Bill asked, interrupting my thoughts.

"My nose is stuffy, I have a headache, and my freakin' leg hurts."

"Hopefully, you only got a mild dose of the virus."

"They're running tests," I said as I tried to quiet the fear in my own heart. "I should know something later, and I'm not ready to panic."

"Well, Captain Harris sends his regards, as does Gabe Petrie."

"Petrie? Really?"

"Yes, he says the whole thing could have been a lot worse if not for you."

"Credit where credit is due. It was that female technician, Julie, who helped convince the team to freeze the electronics."

"In any case, the terrorist attack has been stopped and the bad guys are in custody."

"And I'm the one locked up," I grumbled.

"For your own protection, Len."

"Okay, go clean up the paperwork, and see if you can get my nurse to feed me."

"She seemed annoyed with you."

"That's why I need you to talk to her. Tell her I really did need to sneak out."

"You got it, Len. I'll visit tomorrow."

The nurse did bring me my breakfast, something that was supposed to be an omelette, along with a cup of the weakest coffee known to man. I honestly think a brown crayon in hot water would have been better.

She also took more samples of my blood, urine, et cetera. I think she took pleasure in jabbing the needle in a little harder than necessary.

I then was left alone to think.

That was the worst thing because I *did* think.

I thought about Jyanette, and about how much I loved her. Was getting back together the best thing for *her*, though? I was being selfish, focusing on what I wanted. Was life in Washington better for her? I hadn't known how difficult being a prosecutor had been on her, constantly taking abuse from low-lifes similar to Lindwall and his ilk.

Maybe Calvin had been wrong for her, but maybe I was as well.

That concept stung and made tears come to my eyes, even more than when my nurse stuck me with the needles.

If I truly loved her, I had to face the fact that having me out of her life might be the best thing for her.

I dozed for a while until the phone woke me up.

Jyanette was sitting at the window outside my isolation room, and I picked up the phone.

"Hey, there," she said, forcing a smile.

"Here we go again. Me in a hospital and you visiting me."

"We're both lucky we're alive," she said.

"Yeah." I could barely find any words. The concern in her eyes nailed my heart to my ribs.

"It's given me a chance to think," she said.

"Me, too. A lot."

"Let me say—"

"No, Jyanette, please let me go first."

"Alright."

"I love you, madly and completely — but I've been selfish, wanting you for myself. I can't do it anymore."

She looked at me with a very serious expression. "I see."

"I know how much you hate me getting into these situations, getting hurt. But ever since the night Cathy died—"

"Your fiancée?"

"Yes. Ever since the night she died and I gained these abilities, I have tried to find the purpose as to why I have them. Things like this are the purpose. I can save lives. I can help others. I really have no desire to play hero, but if I am called into a case, it's for a damn good reason."

Jyanette nodded but said nothing.

"And it's not fair to ask you to be part of it. I need to do this, but so far, it has led to misery and loss for you. I can't ask you to do that anymore."

"Len, I—"

"Please let me finish," I interrupted, and took a deep breath. This was the hard part for me. "And I need someone who will be there, no matter what. I need a commitment. Someone who will face the risk and not run away."

Jyanette stared at me, shock on her face. "I didn't run away," she whispered.

"I know, Jyanette… but that's what it felt like to me. I can't go through that with you again. I can't walk on eggshells worried that something I do will frighten you so much that I can't do what I'm needed to do. Losing you ruined me, and I am only getting back to normal now."

She drew a deep breath. "I know how much you love me," she said. "I mean, more than ever, I really do."

"Yes, but I can't keep losing you, and I can't ask you to stay."

Jyanette stared at me through the window, tears glistened in her eyes. "I guess you've made your position clear."

"I had to."

"Then I guess I need to do some thinking, myself," Jyanette said. She gently put the phone back into the handset, and with a glance to me, got up and left the room.

I lay back as the tears flowed from my eyes.

I lay in bed the rest of the day, miserable, and trying to think of what I was going to do when I got out of this place.

My desire to drink had been very subdued since the leg surgery and the painkillers, but it came roaring back as I lay there. If my door hadn't been locked, I might have snuck out to find myself an open bar, even with my ass hanging out the back of my hospital gown.

It was late afternoon when a male doctor came in, masked and gloved, with a clipboard.

"How am I, Doctor?"

"Well, we want to get your surgeon to take a look at your leg. You've obviously been overusing it recently, and I think he'll want to—"

I sat up in bed and all but shouted, "The *virus*, Doctor. Am I sick?"

He was surprised by my reaction, then looked at his clipboard. "Oh? It appears you caught a cold."

"A cold?" I repeated in disbelief.

"Yes, pretty common this time of year. We're going to keep you another night for observation, and your surgeon, Doctor Hirschfeld, wants to take a look at your leg."

I lay back in the bed and started to chuckle.

The young doctor seemed annoyed at this. "Mister Wise, it is very serious to over-stress a leg so soon after a knee replacement."

My chuckle became a rollicking laugh, and the doctor finally gave up, shook his head in disbelief, and left the room.

Kate visited me that evening, soon after I had eaten a dinner almost as tasteless as the breakfast. I think the reason hospital food is so terrible is to encourage a patient to get well and get the hell out.

The phone rang and I saw her through the window.

"Hey, there."

"I heard you caught a cold," Kate said, a grin on her face.

"All that running around outside, I guess."

"We need to talk," she said decisively.

I sighed. "I guess we do."

"These last few months have been fun…"

"Yeah."

"But we have to be honest with each other. I can see how you feel about Jyanette."

"Doesn't matter," I sighed. "She's gone for good this time."

"Even so," Kate said. "I want someone who will look at me the way you look at her. And I know that that will never be you."

"I'm sorry, Kate."

"I'm not. You helped me through a bad time, and made me feel attractive again, feel like a woman instead of a damaged victim. I will always thank you for that."

"You're a beautiful woman, Kate. You deserve a man who will adore you."

"I agree," Kate said and smiled. "I want things to be good between us."

"They are, Kate."

"Good. See you around, Wise."

"You too, Yearling."

The next day, Doctor Irving Hirschfeld came by, lectured me on taking my rehab in stages, and looked at my knee. He decided his work had been brilliant, and that I was coming along ahead of schedule despite overusing the leg.

I was officially released, and Bill met me at the hospital in a police SUV and got me into it. As he drove me home, I had little to say, still locked in my cocoon of misery over losing Jyanette again. When he wheeled me into my sitting room at home, Mrs. Higgins was waiting to take over.

"He's all yours, Mrs. Higgins," Bill said.

"And who else's would he be?" Mrs. Higgins replied.

"By the way, Len, there was a reward on Lindwall," Bill said. "I'm working on the paperwork to get it assigned to you."

"Thanks, Bill," I said in a monotone.

I caught the glance Mrs. Higgins exchanged with Bill.

Mrs. Higgins spoke up. "Well now, that hospital food was dreadful, to be sure. I'll just get ye a nice soup."

Mrs. Higgins fussed over me, and tried to raise my spirits, but it was a fruitless task. I napped in my clothes, ate what she put in front of me, and took my pills, but I was in no mood to be cheered.

I caught up on my email and saw messages from my mentor, Doctor Kohl, but didn't want to read them. With the painkillers, my psychic intuitions were muted anyway, and I decided I would be no help to anyone.

At about eight o'clock, there was a knock at my door. I was at my desk in my wheelchair, with my cane next to me, but I ignored it at first.

The knock repeated, more vigorously.

I moved to the door, annoyed that someone else was coming by to try to lift my spirits.

I opened the door to Jyanette, in her long winter coat. She pushed right past me before I could utter a word, and placed a bag upon my desk. I dutifully shut the door and followed her.

She sat on the corner of my desk with her long coat closed up to her neck and glared at me. "That was a crappy thing to do to me in the hospital."

I sighed. "Jyanette, if you want to yell at me—"

"No, dammit. I want to tell you that I thought about it. I thought about *all* of it."

She stood and yanked off her gloves, but still kept her coat on as she moved to me in the wheelchair. "You're right, I hate you getting hurt and I have gone through a lot of bad stuff since we have known each other. But — I also dealt with being an assistant DA and now an agent of the Department of Justice. Do you know what I learned?"

I was not sure where this was going. "Uh... no?"

"That I like being a lawyer, but I sure as hell don't like dealing with politics. And in Washington, the politics and the politicians are ten times worse than they were in Essex County."

I tried to follow where this was going. "So... you want to change careers?"

"Maybe I want to do something different. Something I feel good about."

"That's... um... great. What do you have in mind?"

"Flipping houses," she announced. "It makes sense, I spent so much time on work sites every summer with my dad."

Jyanette's father, George Emery, was a renowned restorer of historic buildings, and I knew that Jyanette had enjoyed working with him each summer until she received her law degree.

"That sounds like a good idea."

"Yes, it is, and do you know a great place to find undervalued houses and turn them around?"

I, of course, had no idea. "Um… Virginia?"

"Now, you're just being an ass. New Jersey, you dunce."

I couldn't suppress my smile. "You mean it? But, everything you worked for—"

"I thought a lot about what you said," Jyanette affirmed. "You were right. You need someone who will be there for you, who is committed to you. Who will accept you as you are."

"Yes, but—"

"If I'm worried about you going into a dangerous place alone, changing my career will give me the freedom to go with you!"

"What?"

"That is, if Bill or the FBI isn't available."

"Are you sure?"

"That would be the deal, Doctor Wise. If we are going to make this relationship work, you don't face a situation alone. We are a team. You go in with backup or you go in with me. Take it or leave it."

I wanted to pinch myself and make sure I wasn't dreaming. "I-I'll take it."

She grinned. "You're not so dumb after all."

She stood before me and unbuttoned her long coat. I was shocked to find her wearing the silky blue formal dress I had seen only one other time. It clung to her body, showing every curve, and the front revealed just enough cleavage to be provocative without being daring.

She had worn the exact same dress the night we'd been held prisoner at the Blackshale asylum, the same night we'd been at a fund-raiser for Garden State University.

I knew this one had to be a replacement, as the original dress had been ruined from the pair of us fighting for our lives, but wearing that dress had far more meaning, of which only we two were aware.

In a moment of passion, while she wore that dress, the two of us had made love in the shadows not far from the party.

It had been that lovemaking session where Jyanette had unexpectedly become pregnant.

I was speechless to see her in it.

She reached into the paper bag and pulled out a bottle of what looked like champagne.

"What is—?" was all I could manage.

"Relax it's sparkling apple juice, not alcohol. Let me get some glasses."

She sauntered by me, her hips moving sensuously as she went into the bathroom and retrieved a pair of small glasses.

She popped the cork on the bottle. She filled both glasses and handed me one.

"What is all this?" I finally said.

"It's a normal custom, a toast. It's when two people have something to celebrate."

She clinked my glass and took a sip. I sipped as well and stared dumbly at her.

"Leonard Wise, you told me that you were after a commitment."

"I did say that," I replied, still trying to understand all of this.

"That's fair. I love you and I've decided I want to be with you after all, good or bad, no matter what," she said. She pulled her dress up a bit as she lowered herself to one knee so she was eye-level with me in my chair.

"What are you doing?" I asked.

She put a finger over my mouth, and I got the hint to shut up. She took my hand in hers and stared deeply into my eyes, smiling.

"Leonard Wise, will you marry me?"

My mouth fell open.

She waited a moment, then explained, "This is where you say something."

Say something? I wasn't sure this was real, a dream, a vision, or an alien encounter!

"Yes," I finally blurted. "With all my heart, yes."

"Good!" she said and rose. "Now, do you still have that engagement ring?"

I fumbled for a minute, surprised she remembered the ring. "Um... yes... it's in my desk. I didn't return it."

She wheeled me over to the desk and I yanked open drawers until I found the small velvet box and lifted it to her. The tiny solitaire jewel sat in the middle of the gold band. She held out her hand and I placed the ring upon it, and she bent to give me a long and passionate kiss.

She broke the kiss, leaving me in a state of obvious arousal.

"One more thing I have to do," she told me and walked over to the hallway door and flung it open and yelled out, "Margery."

"Aye now, who's that?" I heard from down the hall.

"It's Jyanette, Margery. Len and I are engaged."

There was a 'whoop' that I didn't think Mrs. Higgins was capable of making. "Saints be praised, ye heard me prayers."

"We'll all talk about it in the morning," she yelled back, then looked at me with a smoldering glance. "Right now, I have to consummate the relationship."

"Have fun!" she hollered back.

Jyanette shut the door and turned to me, my head reeling from all that had happened in the last few minutes, and I was so aroused it was painful.

She reached behind herself and unzipped the dress, letting it fall to the floor. She was braless and naked except for a small blue thong and her shoes.

She pushed my chair into the bedroom. I stood and she pulled my clothes off as our lips met.

She kicked off her shoes, rolled onto the bed, hooked her thumbs in the thong to pull it off and looked up at me, beautiful and naked in the dim light of a single lamp.

"Let's see what you can do, now that you have both knees," she challenged.

I pulled off the last of my clothes and joined her.

EPILOGUE

The next day, Mrs. Higgins brought Jyanette and I breakfast in bed, gushing over our engagement. It was difficult as we were both naked, but with the covers hiding us, I have to admit, we were both pretty giddy as well.

We enjoyed our meal, and made love again once we were done eating, and spent most of that day in bed, making love, talking, and getting reacquainted.

That evening, Jyanette brought her luggage to my place, and a day later we realized that she had caught my cold. It wasn't really surprising, with the tension of the previous days, and us swapping spit and all.

Jyanette bought newspapers and searched online for real estate for sale, looking for a bargain. This new idea was beginning to grow on her, and she started to make spreadsheets to figure it all out. I helped any way I could.

We spent most of the next week in bed, indulging our passion for each other as if sex had been our personal invention, and we wanted to explore all of the ways we could indulge in it.

And yes, having two knees that could bend did increase the range of sexual possibilities quite nicely.

During this time, she told me about dating Marcus Calvin, and her job at the DOJ. She also informed me that before coming over to propose, she had tendered her resignation.

"Why did you do that?" I asked.

"I told you, it was really far too political for me. It's time I found my calling, like you did yours."

"Are you sure this is what you really want?"

She smiled at me. "Well, if I'm getting married to a guy in New Jersey, it helps if I'm here."

I had never been happier.

We called our families, let them know about the engagement, and Jyanette told her parents she had to figure out her living situation during the next few weeks.

My mother and father were pleased, they liked Jyanette, and my brother Thomas, who had recently become engaged himself, suggested a double wedding.

Having her there every night and coming home to her from the college every day was like a honeymoon for me. We knew we had to come up with long-term living arrangements, but in the meantime we were both happy.

Two weeks after the last canister had been found, the pair of us attended a funeral, along with the entire Mountainview Police department.

The Federal agents had all gone back to Washington, taking their SWAT teams and portable labs with them. The FBI was represented at the funeral by Gabe Petrie, Kate Yearling, and to my surprise, Agent Calvin.

I heard later through the grapevine that he had requested to be reassigned to the FBI New Jersey Task Force, so I would be seeing him in the future.

As I found my seat and looked over the crowd, Bill and everyone wearing black made me realize again that we had avoided a catastrophe of biblical proportions. I couldn't help but wonder how many would have died if I had not pushed myself to become involved.

I also reflected on the situations that had resulted from having me on the team. Agent Marsh had not been found and was still on the run. What would have happened if he had not been assigned to Calvin who knew Jyanette, who in turn, recommended McGee and me? It felt to me that the universe went out of its way to not only make me part of the investigation, but also to allow Jyanette and me to end up together.

The memorial service was full, but there was no coffin. The body had been cremated, and an urn next to the podium held the remains.

A funeral director asked the people to sit down, and recited a few vapid catchphrases before calling Bill up to the podium.

McGee stood looking over the crowd. "We are here to recognize a member of law enforcement taken from us in an act of terror. I think it best if the one who knew the deceased best were to speak."

Joseph Tice rose and made his way to the podium. He looked pale and weak, only having been released from isolation the previous day, after he was finally free of the virus that had almost killed him.

He went to the podium and faced us all. "I want to thank MPD for coming out. Lanie Woods was a complicated person, who did things that were dangerous, as all of us who chose law enforcement must do. But she had taken an oath and was willing to go undercover and track down people who threatened not only us, but all of the people we watch over every day. She tried to do the right thing, at the cost of her life."

Tice went on for about twenty minutes and I looked at the urn that contained the earthly remains of Lanie. I realized that her own psychic gifts weren't enough to save her from being betrayed by Marsh and killed by Lindwall.

In a sense it was a warning to me, to make sure I paid attention in the real world, and not just think that my second-level abilities would always warn me or save me. They gave me an edge, nothing more.

We sat, with my cane in my right hand to help me walk, the wheelchair no longer needed. I entwined my fingers with Jyanette's, feeling the warmth of her, alive and well, sitting beside me.

I did not know what lay before me, possibly things more terrifying than the last few weeks, but I knew, no matter what storms might be on the horizon, I had Jyanette as my anchor and my partner to keep me grounded and stable.

And I would be hers as well.

FREE PREVIEW

JUSTICE IN THE MIND

DOCTOR WISE BOOK 11

ARJAY LEWIS

MIND
BENDER
PRESS

FREE PREVIEW

Hunched under the harsh gleam of a desk lamp, Alex Worling conversed on the phone. It was one of twenty telephones, their wires snaking across the dim floor of his office.

"Honestly, Mrs. Henderson — I wish there was something we could do." His voice was sickly sweet. "Unfortunately, you have an outstanding tax debt of five thousand dollars, and we have to start enforcement proceedings. This may require police intervention, and we may have to foreclose on your assets, like your home."

As he listened to the elderly woman's rising panic on the phone, a smile graced his lips. She spoke of her deceased husband and the constraints of her income. Her gullibility and naïveté were evident.

Perfect.

"I understand, Mrs. Henderson," Worling said, sympathetically.

This was just too easy. His computer made random phone calls. In an automated voice, it claimed the recipient had unpaid taxes. The recording demanded immediate contact with an agent or face police intervention. Most people just hung up, but now and then he got a live one.

"I could use Form 2289—" Worling said, making up the number, "—for extreme situations, like yours. If you can pay the first five hundred dollars on a credit card, I might clear this up for you today."

"Oh? Can you do that?" she responded hopefully.

Of course, he could take her money. He would demand the five-hundred-dollar fee. Then he would produce a copy of her card to use for several days. Eventually, the credit card company would detect the forgery and deactivate the account.

Who was he hurting? The credit card company had insurance, and the elderly woman would hopefully learn to be more cautious.

"I'm authorized to commit to a settlement right now, and we can clear this all up."

"Well, my husband took care of all this, but since he died…" the old woman said.

An unexpected knocking on the office door made Worling look up and furrow his brow. No one knew he would be here, and visitors were exceedingly rare.

"As I was saying, all I need is your credit card number—"

A second knock echoed through the room.

"Excuse me, Mrs. Henderson, my supervisor is knocking on my cubicle. I have to make sure he will approve this settlement before I continue. Let me put you on hold, please."

He placed the receiver on the desk. This was his skill, the adeptness of a seasoned swindler. He seamlessly incorporated an unexpected interruption into his narrative and used it.

A master of his craft, that's what he was.

He cautiously opened the door, limited by the constraints of the security chain.

"Yeah, who is it? Whaddya want?"

The hallway was not well lit, and the man was tall, in a long dark leather coat with a black felt fedora perched on his head, leaving his face in shadows. He spoke in a deep voice, "Mr. Worling?"

"Yeah, I'm Worling. What about it?"

"You killed Willard Johnson eight years ago, during a robbery."

"What are you, a reporter or somethin'? Look, that was manslaughter, and I served my time for it."

"Five years for killing a man," the tall guy said.

Worling was glad he'd gotten the heavy-duty security chain. This guy was creeping him out.

"Go complain to the judge. I'm busy here," Worling said as he closed the door and turned the heavy deadbolt in place.

An explosion ripped through the middle of the thick oak panels, shattering the door.

It threw Alex to the ground, as pain shot through his back and he cried out in agony. With trembling hands, he touched his back and his fingers came away with a gory display of blood.

Three men surged into the room through the broken door. One of them wore a ski mask and the other one was bald and chunky, carrying a heavy-duty battering ram. The one in the fedora stood over him, holding an enormous gun with a suppressor on the barrel.

He aimed the gun at Worling's face. It looked like it was the size of a cannon.

The man with the gun spoke again. "After murdering an innocent man, you now steal from people with your scams. And we know about your other plans."

"What... the..." Worling said, struggling to breathe. "I need... a hospital."

"You don't need a hospital. Your time is up."

"What do you want?" Worling begged.

"Justice," said the big man as he squeezed the trigger.

TO BE CONTINUED IN

JUSTICE IN THE MIND

DOCTOR WISE BOOK 11

AUTHOR'S NOTE

Hello, follower of the odd. (Sounds a little like I have my own cult!)

Infection In the Mind is an action-packed ride counterpointed by Len being in a wheelchair for most of the book.

I wrote the rough draft in November 2020 and released the book in March 2021, when we were all in pandemic mode. Even though the idea of a biological agent was the dominant theme, it wasn't because of the actual events. I had planned *Infection* back in 2017 when I created my Doctor Wise timeline that sketched out the series to eighteen books. I always intended for it to be the tenth book, and I always planned to incorporate the threat of an infectious bioweapon.

The real-world situation was merely a coincidence.

I also intended it to be the book that threw Len and Jyanette back together again. Despite all the challenges they have faced, I wanted them to be a couple. I am, at heart, a hopeless romantic, and I believe in love. Maybe it doesn't conquer all, but it makes our trip through this lifetime better.

And sometimes you find the perfect person to share that journey. The journey will continue with the next book, *Justice In The Mind.*

—Arjay Lewis

ABOUT THE AUTHOR

K nown as the "Wizard Of Odd," Arjay Lewis is an actor, magician, and multi-award-winning author.

I write tales of the strange and the horrifying.

I have spent my life as an entertainer, amusing people as a street-performer in the 1970s; a Broadway and casino artist in the 1980s; a party performer in the 1990s and 2000s; a cruise ship performer in the 2010s.

Stories have always been in my mind, and I have been writing since the 1990s. My reason to write is simple: to entertain. I write the type of books that I like to read: murder mysteries, strange tales of unnatural gifts, odd happenings and horror.

Please visit my web site and sign up for my mailing list to be "in the know" for upcoming books. Visit me on Facebook, Twitter, or my Amazon Author page.

And thank you for reading. You are the reason I write.

www.arjaylewis.com
www.facebook.com/arjaylewis
www.twitter.com/arjaylewiswrite
www.amazon.com/Arjay-Lewis